Praise for Cat Johnson's
Ride

"...if you like hard headed strippers, Vegas and cowboys, grab Cat's book, settle back with some popcorn and devour this yummy read!"

~ *PNR Reviews*

"Ride is a brilliant addition to Cat Johnson's Studs in Spurs series...Ms. Johnson instills the perfect amount of sexual tension, surprising twists, uncertainty and longing throughout Ride so the plot flows beautifully and leaves the reader with a sense of hopefulness and joy and at times even sadness."

~ *Romance Junkies*

"This is a new-to-me author, and after reading this delightful story, it won't be the last. I was drawn in by Ms. Johnson's humorous, emotional story. If you enjoy a hot romance, humor, and a book you won't forget, then come along for the ride."

~ *Whipped Cream Reviews*

Look for these titles by *Cat Johnson*

Now Available:

Rough Stock

Studs in Spurs Series
Unridden
Bucked
Ride
Hooked

Red, Hot and Blue Series
Trey
Jack
Jimmy
Jared
Cole

Ride

Cat Johnson

SAMHAIN
PUBLISHING

Samhain Publishing, Ltd.
11821 Mason Montgomery Road, 4B
Cincinnati, OH 45249
www.samhainpublishing.com

Ride
Copyright © 2011 by Cat Johnson
Print ISBN: 978-1-60928-309-4
Digital ISBN: 978-1-60928-262-2

Editing by Heidi Moore
Cover by Angie Waters

First Samhain Publishing, Ltd. electronic publication: December 2010
First Samhain Publishing, Ltd. print publication: November 2011

Dedication

Dedicated to the real-life inspiration for Chase, whose youthful exuberance has picked me up when I'm down and filled my author's brain with hot cowboys to share with you all. Without him, Slade, Mustang and Chase may never have been created. For Mike.

A special thanks goes to Tammy for her ideas on how to "dirty up" my innocent Chase a bit.

Finally, to Dr. Wicked, whose evil genius and "Write or Die" program prodded this procrastinating writer into unsurpassed productivity.

As usual, any mistakes made or liberties taken with the facts in this work of fiction are purely my own.

Chapter One

She arrived at work early, as usual, and opened her locker. A white envelope floated to the ground. She bent to retrieve it. *Leesa Santiago* was scrawled in ink across the front.

Good. Her boss had finally paid them on time for once, which was fortunate since her rent was due. Though it seemed her rent was always due, or the cell phone bill, or the monthly credit card payment on the huge balance left by her son-of-a-bitch ex boyfriend. It was no surprise her checking account was always empty. Everything in Vegas cost a lot. Far more than it had in the small town where she'd grown up in Washington state.

Smothering any nostalgia for home, Leesa tore into the envelope. Her blood pressure shot sky high when she saw the laughably low total on the check. She slammed the locker door with enough force to rattle the entire row of attached metal cabinets. She'd had enough.

Leesa stomped her way to her boss's door and flung it open without knocking. She ignored the man seated across from Jerry. Hell, she barely even noticed the stacks of cash on the desk between them. Instead she focused on the piece of slime who thought he could pay her whatever he felt like, regardless of how many shifts she worked for him. "Jerry. What the hell? You shorted my pay *again*."

"Fuck." Beneath the chock of overly-gelled black hair hanging low on his forehead, Jerry's shifty eyes cut from her, to the man seated on the other side of the desk with his back to her, then back to Leesa. "Can't you see I'm busy? I don't have time for your shit."

Standing her ground, Leesa opened her mouth to protest when Jerry cut her off before she got another word out. "Get the fuck out of here. Now!"

With an angry huff, she spun and slammed the door hard behind her.

"Frigging bastard. Son of a bitch..." Her steady stream of uncomplimentary names for him lasted all the way back to the lockers where her coworker Holly was dressing in her costume for the night.

Holly glanced up from tying the laces on her thigh-high boots. "Jerry?"

"Yeah." Leesa let out a bitter laugh that there was really no question about who could make her that angry before the work night had even begun. "He shorted my paycheck again."

Finished fussing with the boot, Holly planted her black patent-leather heel on the dingy linoleum floor and straightened. She glanced at her reflection as she adjusted her boobs inside the black vinyl corset.

Leesa marveled once again at how opposite they were.

Holly was a platinum blonde with larger-than-life hair sprayed until it didn't move no matter how energetically she danced or how shitty the air conditioner performed. Her blue eyes were always accentuated with even bluer shadow and lots of black liner and thick long eyelashes. Usually there was some sort of shimmer on her cheeks to "bounce the stage lights," as Holly would say.

On the other hand, Leesa was like the darker, less glittery

version of Holly. Her long, straight brown hair was either pulled into a high ponytail or braid, and always sans hairspray so it would move. The men seemed to like when she swung it around dramatically while she danced. Holly said that was probably an instinct left over from caveman days when they used to dance in front of the cave fire and drag women around by their hair. That theory had given them both a chuckle. Plenty of customers they dealt with were no better than Neanderthals.

Leesa glanced at her own reflection again. Before tonight's performance she would accent her green eyes with just enough brown liner and mascara so Holly wouldn't yell at her for not wearing *proper* stage makeup. Poor Holly tried so hard to help, but the truth was it was a good day if Leesa remembered to sweep on blush at all, forget about glitter.

As Holly applied more makeup on top of what she was already wearing, her gaze moved to meet Leesa's in the mirror. "I don't know why you bother complaining. He's just going to say we work for tips and are lucky he pays us anything at all for a shift."

Leesa opened her locker for the second time that night and angrily shoved the envelope into her purse. "I don't care if we do make tips too. He should pay what he owes us for the shift. We're the ones up on stage bringing in the customers while he sits back there on his ass counting piles of money."

Holly turned and leaned against the low counter covered with tubes and bottles of makeup with a few hair accessories mixed in. "I've worked other places, sweetie. Believe me. Things could be a whole lot worse than Jerry shorting you a shift here or there."

She scowled. "I don't know how this job could get any worse."

"Oh, hon. Trust me, it could." Holly shook her head. "Jerry

ever make you have sex with him or his friends to keep your job?"

"No." Leesa swallowed away the bitter taste that idea brought.

"He ever try and get you hooked on drugs?"

Leesa shook her head. "No. All that stuff happens?"

"Oh, yeah. Not a lot, but far too often for my liking. Take my advice. Don't make waves. Do what I do. Come in, dance, collect the tips and go home. You'll be a lot happier and safer that way."

The word *safer* stuck out glaringly amid the rest. Drawing in a deep breath, Leesa hoped she could stomp down the residual resentment she still harbored against Jerry and do her job. In spite of the enlightening talk with Holly, Leesa still hated the man with a passion. She let the air out in a whoosh.

"All right. I'll try." Leesa didn't have time to obsess about Jerry right now anyway. The show must go on. She wasn't wearing a watch, but she figured the girls on the day shift would be done in less than an hour and then she'd be up. Leesa stared at the outfits lined up on hangers inside her locker. Choosing seemed beyond her in her current state. Frustrated, she turned to Holly. "What the hell should I wear?"

Holly laughed. "If that is the biggest thing we both have to worry about tonight, I'll be a happy girl. Now, what should you wear? I'm not sure why, but there've been a lot of cowboys around here this weekend. Boots, hats, slow-as-molasses sexy southern drawls, the works. I'm thinking you might want to go with your Pocahontas outfit."

"A cowboys and Indians theme?" Leesa let out a snort and pulled the fringed faux suede mini skirt out of the locker. "Sure, why not. Are cowboys good tippers?"

"Eh. That usually depends how well they did in the casino.

I love me some cowboys. Of course, it could just be that I've got a thing for a man wearing a hat and boots. It's even better when he's wearing not much else. Comes from growing up in Texas, I guess." Holly leaned toward the mirror and applied another layer of bright red lipstick. "Some of the guys last night sure were cute."

Leesa watched, not sure whether Holly's ever-present sexy pout was natural or medically enhanced. All she knew was she didn't have the money herself for cosmetic improvements to any part of her body, no matter how small the body part or the enhancement. What she had was what God had given her. The customers could either take it or leave it. She had no choice either way.

Feeling her current poverty intensely, and hating Jerry all over again for his small part in it, Leesa sighed. "Cute doesn't pay the rent, Holly."

In fact, *cute* was the reason she was here stripping instead of in some great job somewhere using the college diploma she'd never gotten a chance to finish earning because she'd fallen for *cute.*

"I told you how you can make more money." Holly broke her gaze away from her own reflection, glanced around the room and then leaned closer toward Leesa. "I covered half of my rent for the entire month just with what I earned last night with a few special lap dances in the back room. That's another reason I like it here at Jerry's—doors on the back room instead of just curtains. All the privacy a girl could want for making a little extra."

They'd talked about this before. Leesa knew it wasn't only lap dances that happened in that back room. For a few bills thrown their way at the end of the shift, the bouncers would be there in an emergency if you needed them, but otherwise they would basically turn a blind eye to anything else that happened between the girls and the customers, whether it was against the rules or not.

"I know, Holly. I just…I thought I could get by on my pay and tips. I didn't think I'd have to do anything…more."

The other woman's attention returned to her own reflection, this time checking the rear view as she adjusted the G-string and black micro miniskirt covering her lower half. "That's your choice, hon, but really, why are you killing yourself? A few hand jobs a night and all your financial troubles would be over."

"Just hand jobs?" Doubtful, Leesa raised a brow.

Holly shrugged. "Sure, if that's all you want to do."

"Is that all the rest of the girls do?" Was she seriously considering doing this? Then again, she'd just stripped down to absolutely nothing so she could don a G-string and a skimpy Pocahontas costume, all so she could walk out in front of a bunch of strange men and take it off again on stage. How had her life gotten so messed up?

Holly met Leesa's gaze in the dressing room's mirror again. "No."

"Yeah, I didn't think so." Leesa pulled the fringed vest over her bare breasts and stared at her own reflection. She looked a world away from when she was a starry-eyed college student in California who'd been stupid enough to fall in love. Who was she kidding? She might as well be a world away. Life in Las Vegas was like another planet compared to what she used to know.

"Listen. Try it once. If you don't like it, don't do it again." Holy shrugged, as if she were talking about Leesa tasting some new food she was reluctant to sample. "You call all the shots, you know. You pick which guys. You choose how far it goes."

"And they'd be okay with that? Me choosing how far it

14

goes?" Leesa's stomach fluttered with...what? She wasn't sure. Nerves caused by even thinking of doing what Holly suggested maybe?

After Holly wiped a smear of lipstick off her teeth, she turned toward Leesa. "Oh yeah. Usually they're grateful and extremely generous for any extra attention at all in that area. If they're not, call one of the bouncers. Like I said, you're in charge."

You're in charge... Leesa hadn't felt in charge of anything, including her own life, in what seemed like a very long time. Maybe the emotion sending her stomach into flips was anticipation, not nervousness.

She could choose. Who. When. How far.

Damn, the idea of having power was enticing. Addictive almost. She liked it. A lot.

Chapter Two

Intermission was coming to an end and the fans were starting to retake their seats for the championship round. Chase Reese carried his most recent purchase down the long, relatively quiet hall toward the noise and action in the arena. The weight of the new rope felt right in his hand. The rattling of the old cowbell was a comfortingly familiar sound though the bull rope itself was still kind of strange.

Even if he had convinced himself he didn't give a crap about the other guys' opinions when he'd invested in a new rope right before the finals, he still needed it to feel like his. Each ride made it seem more familiar, more his own, and gave him more confidence he'd made the right decision. He'd needed to shake things up a bit to get him out of his slump.

Most of the riders he knew used the same bull rope until it was in tattered shreds, because they were afraid to make any changes to their gear that might somehow affect their concentration or their riding.

Bull riders could be a superstitious bunch. Some had rituals they did the same exact way before every ride. Others avoided wearing certain colors when riding. Chase scowled at that idea. If simply putting on a yellow shirt meant a wreck while a red shirt equaled a ninety-point ride, this sport would be easy.

He didn't believe in that superstitious crap, but he couldn't spend as many hours a day as he did with these guys and not have some of what they thought rub off on him. He'd seen a few sympathetic looks and judgmental shakes of their heads when he walked into the arena with his pristinely new bull rope two nights ago. Worse, Chase knew some small seed of doubt had stuck with him all the way until his ass had hit the bull's back and he'd wrapped that new rope around his glove that first night. Most every rider except for Mustang Jackson thought he was asking for trouble by changing ropes before the biggest competition of the year.

As he walked, Chase glanced down at the rope, now tinged with rosin and dirt, and realized his decision had been correct. His new spurs, another fairly recent purchase, jangled with every step of his boots hitting the ground. Further testament that what Mustang had told him was true. It wasn't what you did or wore that put you on top. It was what you did on top of the bull that mattered. This competition Chase must be doing something right. His name listed high up on the leader board clearly showed that.

That thought put an added little spring in his step as he exited the long hallway between the locker room and the arena and the full force of the sold-out event hit him.

Pausing in the area behind the chutes, Chase flipped his rope over the top rail and took a moment to look around. The packed sports center, the noise of the crowd, the television cameras and crew—it could easily overwhelm a twenty-two-year-old kid from Oklahoma. Chase simply couldn't let it get under his skin. Sometimes that was easier said than done.

The sound of boots and spurs directly behind him had Chase turning to see his friend Garret approaching. "One more ride then we're done for this season. You know what that means, don't you?"

17

"I get to be home for more than a few days in a row before I have to leave again?" Living on the road was fun, but there was something to be said for Mama's cooking. And Chase missed his older brother.

"Well, yeah. But it also means we can get wild tonight because we don't have to ride or even travel tomorrow." Garret grinned.

Chase nodded. "Yup. I guess it does. What d'ya wanna do?"

"I wanna do anything and everything. This is Vegas, baby! We can stay up all night and sleep all day tomorrow if we want." With the scrape of metal on metal, Garret leaned back and hooked the spurred heel of one boot on the bottom rail.

"Not exactly. We've got that charity event tomorrow. Remember?" Chase laughed at the stricken expression on Garret's face. "Don't act like it's the end of the world. I'm still looking forward to downing a few cold ones the minute we're done riding here tonight."

This being the last competition before their break, they could afford to do some major destruction to their bodies partying for a night or two—Chase would have plenty of time to hit the gym when he got home to Oklahoma—but they couldn't miss the fan event or they'd be in big trouble.

"I was planning on getting totally shitfaced tonight myself. Damn. I forgot all about that meet-and-greet thing tomorrow. It was your birthday yesterday and we didn't get to celebrate hard because we had to ride today."

"We did spend some quality time at that all-you-can-eat buffet. That was good." Chase had gone to bed happy and fuller than a hog.

"I know, but tonight I thought we could really take you out in style." Garret's pout was worthy of any five-year-old who'd just been told he couldn't have his own way.

18

"Garret, we can still go out. We just can't get so annihilated we won't wake up for tomorrow." Chase knew damn well the fans had paid a ton of money, all of which was going to a good cause, just to meet him and the other riders at tomorrow's charity autograph-signing event. That didn't mean he and Garret couldn't indulge in a beer or two tonight though.

"Yeah, you're right I guess. You think Skeeter's fake ID will work here?" As he spoke, Garret's gaze followed the progress of a girl in tight jeans as she climbed the stairs until she finally took her seat.

Chase gave the object of Garret's attention a quick perusal and decided the back view had been superior to the front. Besides, she looked about seventeen, maybe eighteen. Chase preferred girls with a little life experience under their belt, and a bit less beer belly there too.

He wasn't opposed to curves. He just preferred they be in other places besides a beer gut. Generous hips, lush thighs, a nice round butt, tits that made a man take notice, those were all very good things, but he couldn't think too much about that now. He had a ride to prepare for and plans to make with Garret.

He turned his attention back to Garret's question. "I don't know about Skeeter. They're a little more careful about checking IDs here than at the usual bars we hang out at. If it doesn't work, we'll just pick up some supplies and drink in the room."

Garret's mouth twisted at that. "Yeah, but there ain't no chicks up in our room."

Chase laughed. "There will be if you invite them."

His friend grinned in response. "I like how you think."

Accepting Garret's compliment with a nod, Chase glanced around the area behind the chutes. They were getting close to starting the final round. The Brazilians were off to one side warming up and stretching. Some of the others were busy getting their gear ready.

A few of the veteran riders emerged from out of the locker room. Mustang Jackson positioned himself behind the chutes next to Slade Bower. Both began working the rosin into their ropes in preparation for the upcoming ride. It reminded Chase he should be doing the same. He turned back to the rail and grabbed the dangling section of his bull rope. With his glove, he started rubbing up and down the portion of its length he'd later wrap around his hand.

"I suppose we can do a few shots up in our room, then go down to the casino and see what, or who, is around." Garret followed Chase's example, turning toward the rail to prep his own rope.

"Sounds good to me." As Chase worked the rosin into the rope, making it sticky for a better grip during the ride, the announcer's amplified voice reverberated off the walls and ceiling of the cavernous space.

The stock handlers ran the bulls for the first flight of the championship round into the chutes and Chase felt the now familiar surge of adrenaline begin to rush into his bloodstream.

Garret glanced over his shoulder in the direction of the girl he'd been watching before. "Ya think if we ask her to come back to our room with us she'd say yes?"

"I guess." Chase shrugged, not at all interested in that particular girl. He looked up and found Garret frowning at him. "What?"

"You don't sound very enthusiastic."

Probably because Garret would talk about girls twenty-four hours a day if he let him. Chase had learned to nod and agree with Garret without really listening too closely.

"Sorry. I guess I'm just focused on the ride." Not to mention he and Garret usually had pretty much the opposite taste in women. Chase liked sophisticated ladies. Bimbos turned Garret on, unless there were special circumstances like a few too many post-ride shots with the guys. In that case, all bets were off on whom Garret would go for. Case in point, last year in Tulsa when Garret had come home from a bar with the phone number of a woman he normally wouldn't have looked at twice.

The girl in the stands wasn't doing anything for Chase, but she was obviously doing it for his friend. Garret glanced at her again before focusing his attention on Chase. "Ya know, Chase, I really hope you're not still interested in that author chick."

"Jenna? No, of course I'm not." Where the hell had that question come from? Chase had been interested, but that was a year ago. A year to the day to be precise. He'd met her on the night of his birthday during last year's finals, and shortly thereafter discovered she was dating Slade Bower, a fellow bull rider with a jealous streak a mile wide and the fists to back it up.

"I saw you talking to her last night."

Chase let out a short laugh at Garret's suspicion. "Yeah, so? You've been texting Jenna's friend Barb all year."

Garret's brow rose in doubt. "Yeah, but that's just texting. She's not showing up at any of the competitions. And Jenna's writing that book about you."

"Jenna and I are just friends, and the book's not about me exactly. It's just a romance novel based on a rookie bull rider. She's a writer. That's what she does. Write. Doesn't mean she's in love with me or anything. She just thought it was a good story."

"Yeah, whatever." Garret shook his head and went back to his rope.

"Whatever," Chase echoed. He needed some new friends. He also needed to get moving because his bull had just been loaded. He unlooped his rope from the rail. "See ya in a few."

"Need me to help?"

"Nah, looks like Skeeter is already up there. You got a ride coming up yourself to get ready for."

"All right. Try not to eat too much dirt when you fall off." Garret grinned.

Chase laughed. "Yeah, you too."

The cowbell attached to his bull rope hit the dirt with a clanging *thunk*. Chase wound the excess length around his hand and headed toward the chute. As he neared, the bull inside reared and rattled the rails. Chase's level of adrenaline kicked a notch higher.

He set one knee to the ground and said a quick, silent prayer for a safe ride for both himself and the bull, then climbed up. After handing his rope to a stock handler, he pulled his mouth guard from his vest pocket and slipped it between his teeth.

Mentally Chase reviewed how the ride would go. The bull was loaded for a left-hand delivery out of the gate, which would likely mean the animal would spin first to the left and into Chase's riding hand. If Chase kept spurring him with his outside leg, the bull would hopefully not reverse directions. He'd have to stay on top of his rope, try not to slip into the well and keep his eyes off the ground. A lot to think about during a bone-jostling eight seconds when any thought at all was difficult. Piece of cake.

Straddling the metal rails, he lowered himself onto the back of the antsy animal.

Skeeter leaned over and helped pull the rope tight so Chase could wrap it around his gloved left hand. With his weight centered on the animal's bony back, he was ready.

"Chase Reese aboard Moonwalk. This is one rank bull, ridden only twice in ten outs this series."

As Chase heard the announcer speak his name and talk about the upcoming ride, he felt the usual thrill he never experienced at any other time in his life, not even when he was with a woman.

Still amazed he got to do what he loved for a living, Chase felt like the luckiest man on earth. With a surge of pride, he realized he never wanted to do anything else and then nodded to the gate man.

Chapter Three

All dressed up and with nowhere to go until their shift began, Leesa and Holly each grabbed a cup of coffee from the pot always on behind the bar. Back in the dressing room, they sipped the bracing caffeine out of paper hot cups and continued talking about everything and nothing, killing time until the start of another long work night.

One of the day shift girls breezed in amid a cloud of perfume and interrupted their conversation, but not Leesa's serious consideration of what they'd discussed earlier. Holly's solution to Leesa's financial problems tantalized her.

"Hey, Holly. Hey, Leesa. The two new girls aren't here yet?"

Holly scowled and shook her head. "Nope. They'll wander in late as usual."

"Then I guess you two are up. I'm done for the day and Tiffany is just finishing now. Oh, and you've got a birthday boy out there so you're gonna need the handcuffs. Tiff will point him out to you."

Holly grinned, grabbing a pair of furry cuffs out of her locker. "I do love a birthday boy."

Leesa couldn't say she loved their birthday-boy routine, but it was a fun change from the usual. At this point, after strutting up and down that stage for months, anything different was good, she supposed.

She followed Holly out. The fringe of the short skirt hit her bare ass cheeks with every step she took.

Up on the stage, Tiffany was collecting the discarded pieces of her costume and the last of her tips. As the music changed she made her way back toward Leesa and Holly. She paused in front of them with a fist full of singles. "The shy guy in the big white hat has a birthday. His friend said to give him everything we've got, including the back room. The rest of the guys are paying. Wish I could stick around, but I gotta pick up my kid from the sitter."

"That's okay. We'll take good care of him." Holly glanced at the loud group of about half a dozen cowboys and smiled at Leesa. "You wanna take him in the back later?"

"What?" Leesa spun to face Holly then couldn't help but look back at the cowboy in question.

"Come on. It's perfect. He's painfully young by the looks of him. Probably never had a lap dance in his life. He'll be the perfect guy for you to cut your teeth on."

"My teeth?" Leesa gasped at that suggestion.

"Relax. I didn't mean use your teeth literally, unless you want to of course. It's just an expression. I meant he's perfect for your first foray into making a little extra cash. Look at him. He'll probably come the minute the air touches his thing. The young ones finish real fast if they're not too drunk. If he is, well then you may be in for a long haul. But he's cute. It wouldn't be that bad spending some extra time on him."

Leesa glanced in their direction again and tried to estimate how long they'd been there and how much they'd consumed. She realized what she was doing and dragged her gaze away. She couldn't seem to tell Holly no, mainly because she was still seriously considering going through with it.

"You wanna think about it? No pressure. I do love me some

cowboys. Looks like there are plenty to go around, but I'll be glad to take him back if you don't want to." Holly paused and waited for an answer while eyeing the group of young men and practically drooling.

A bouncer had already put a chair up on the stage. They needed to get up there and start the show. Leesa took another look at the group of men in the birthday party, downing beers and laughing. Could she go through with what Holly wanted her to? Did she have another choice? Maybe she could get a shift at a local restaurant to make more money. Maybe she was being foolish, just like Holly said. What was just a few minutes in the back? What happened and with who would be her choice. She could pay off her bills and save enough to go back to college and finish her degree.

What was she worried about? She was safe enough in the club. Glancing back at the cowboy, she saw again that he didn't look like the dangerous type.

Even as it felt like a rock had landed with a thud in her stomach, Leesa shook her head. "That's okay. You don't have to take him, Holly. I'll do it."

She tried to swallow away the sudden dryness in her throat.

Holly grinned. "Good for you. Now come on. It's show time."

They had done this birthday show dozens of times in Leesa's months at the strip club. Usually one man was just like another. She never paid very close attention to them as individuals, but as Holly led their subject onto the stage by the hand, Leesa found herself really studying this one.

Obviously embarrassed, he shook his head and pulled against Holly's grasp. He made a half-hearted attempt to sit back down with the other guys rather than be dragged into the spotlight. Even as he laughed off the ribbing from the other guys, there was a look on his face that said he'd rather be an observer than the center of attention, especially when Holly pushed him into the chair on stage. His Adam's apple bobbed wildly in his throat as Holly cuffed his wrists behind the back of the chair.

Holly started the show, circling him like an animal sizing up its prey while the crowd cheered. Even under the bright spotlights that washed out all but the most intense colors, Leesa could see his face grow red.

His surprise was nearly palpable when Holly whipped off her corset and her breasts bounced just inches in front of his face. Then Holly turned away from him to face the admiring crowd and started to strut toward the far end of the stage, leaving the cowboy alone in the chair watching her leave. He looked almost relieved she had walked away and taken the attention off him.

Poor guy. Little did he know that was Leesa's cue to join the routine. After climbing the stairs onto the stage, Leesa circled the chair. Holly returned and they stalked him together, while the expression on the poor guy's face became almost comical, a cross between embarrassment and anticipation, as though he wasn't sure if what was to come would be good or bad.

Somehow his shyness emboldened Leesa. Standing facing him, she bent from the waist, giving the crowd a nice shot of her ass. The whistles and calls from the audience clearly showed their appreciation. Bracing a hand on each one of his knees, she yanked his thighs apart and spread his legs wide. His eyes flew open at the action. She laughed and a feeling of power surged through her.

Up close he looked a few years younger than her own age. He was probably right off the farm, here in Sin City for one wild night. She could give him that. A night he'd never forget. She liked that idea.

Donning a smile, she leaned in closer to his ear so he would hear her over the noise. "Relax, cowboy. Enjoy it."

He jumped when she spoke. She pulled back enough to see his deer-in-headlights stare as it focused on her face. He swallowed hard again and then nodded. "Yes, ma'am."

She smiled at his down-home politeness even in this situation as she straightened up. He was as sweet as he'd first appeared. Leesa liked that he looked so innocent and squeaky clean. For some reason it made her want to dirty him up a little. Now that she'd wrapped her head around giving him something to remember tonight by in the back room, she was really starting to get into it.

Stepping into the space she'd created between his knees, she turned her back toward him and whipped off her skirt. She jiggled her butt cheeks in front of his face to the accompanying whoops of the other cowboys. Leesa couldn't resist glancing over her shoulder. Mouth slightly agape, he stared mesmerized directly at her ass. Her gaze dropped and yeah, other parts of him had taken notice of her too. That was clearly outlined in his jeans, and she had to admit, it appeared pretty impressive from where she stood.

As Leesa strained to watch over her shoulder, Holly stepped up behind him and ran both of her hands down the front of his shirt, then started to unbutton it. Holly tugged it from where it had been tucked neatly inside his belted jeans and pushed the shirt open to expose a nearly hairless chest. He was lean but definitely fit judging by the sharply cut outline of his chest and stomach muscles.

Meanwhile, the cowboy squirmed in his chair beneath the scrutiny.

Turning to face him fully again, Leesa planted her costume's high-heeled fringed suede boot on the edge of the chair between his thighs. His gaze dropped to the long expanse of her exposed leg in front of him. Visually, he followed the line of her thigh up to the glittering G-string that covered what the law said had to be covered, but not much else.

While Holly took another turn around the stage and collected some more dollar bills, Leesa took the show to the next level. Straddling the blushing cowboy, she ground against him. The only thing separating them was her G-string, the denim of his jeans and whatever underwear he was wearing. She couldn't stop wondering exactly what kind that was. She supposed she'd find out soon enough.

Gyrating her hips, she felt the bulge in his jeans personally. Leesa watched his quick intake of breath at the contact. She couldn't help her own gasp when the friction of rubbing against him caused nerve endings long ignored to wake up. Now that her sex drive had been pulled out of hibernation, it screamed for attention.

She met his gaze and felt her own cheeks grow warm. Their faces were so close, he must have noticed her getting flushed.

In spite of the public venue and the fact it was supposed to be all for show, it somehow became an intimate moment. Leesa shook that thought from her head. She hadn't been with a man since she finally broke it off with her rotten ex. She hadn't even looked at a man with romantic or sexual interest since then because she'd been so turned off after him. She was turned on now though.

The loud whoops from his group of friends in particular served as a very real reminder she was here to entertain the crowd, so entertain she did. Leesa whipped the two sides of her vest apart just inches from the cowboy's face.

Beneath the rim of his hat, his baby blue eyes followed the action before coming back up to meet hers. For a moment time seemed to stand still. It was like they were no longer under the hot spotlights in a crowded, noisy room. A crazy image crashed into her mind of staring into those eyes as he braced above her in her bed. Need coiled within her, poised and begging for release.

Her body was simply reacting with raw animal instinct. He was a desirable male specimen, and she was a woman who hadn't been with one of those in a while. That explained the spreading warmth she felt between her legs. She pressed one last time against the bulge beneath the rough denim before she rose and turned toward the audience.

She may be playing to the crowd for tips at the moment, but Leesa remembered her promise to Holly. Soon she'd be getting up close and personal with this man. Very soon. She tried not to let the unwanted lusty thoughts about this stranger scare the hell out of her. Last time she'd felt this way about a man and let other parts besides her brain do the thinking she'd made the worst decision of her life. She'd ended up dropping out of college in her senior year. That led to her being here now, mostly nude on stage in front of a bar full of men and about to take one of them back to a private room to earn some cash by pleasuring him.

The thought lodged a lump of fear in her heart even as her stomach fluttered at the idea of being alone with him—intimate with him—a man who blushed and called her ma'am and at the same time had her absolutely saturated with desire after one glance into his baby blues. Not to mention the temptation of what was contained within those jeans.

Leesa put some space between herself and the cowboy by doing a lap around the stage. As large, sweaty hands shoved bills into the feather-covered garter around her thigh, she couldn't resist one more glance back at the birthday boy on stage. Leesa also couldn't stop her heart from picking up speed when she realized that even though Holly was dancing directly in front of him, his gaze had followed her.

The song came to an end and so did the birthday routine. One song per customer. That was Jerry's rule, mainly because a customer who was up on stage was not down on the floor ordering overpriced drinks. It was time for the private, behind-closed-doors portion of the evening.

Amid the whoops and cheers of the crowd, she steeled her nerves but couldn't quiet her racing heart as she walked to where the cowboy still sat. From behind Holly uncuffed him from the chair. He didn't move except to bring his hands around front and rub where the cuffs had been. The sleeves of his shirt were rolled up to reveal strong forearms. Then Leesa noticed the red lines on his wrists, as if he'd pulled against the restraints. In spite of the fur on the metal, the cuffs had marked him.

"Are your wrists okay? Do they hurt?" She shifted her gaze from his injuries to his face and saw him smile.

"Hurt? Nah. This is nothing." He shook his head and laughed, a sound that sent warmth coursing through her.

Leesa swallowed hard. It was now or never. "Okay. Good, because your buddies are treating you to one more birthday surprise."

"They are?" His voice squeaked a bit with the question. She smiled.

"Yup." Reaching down, she grabbed one of his arms. His skin felt warm and slightly rough from a fine layer of hair.

He rose willingly when she tugged him from the chair. "What kind of surprise?"

Swallowing hard past the lump in her throat, she pictured

31

that surprise. "It wouldn't be a surprise if I told you."

One handed, he attempted to pull the open sides of his shirt closed and button them while they walked. She shot him a sideways look as she led him down the stairs. "Don't bother. I'm just going to undo it again."

His eyebrows shot up beneath the brim of his hat and she swore his cheeks got pinker than before. "Oh."

Laughing, she pulled him toward the back.

A bouncer nodded to her as she went past and into one of the private rooms, which really shouldn't be called a room at all since it was more the size of closet. It contained a chair and not much more. Someone had left a box of tissues on the floor next to the chair. The sight of that made it all seem more real. She pulled the door closed behind her and heard it latch with a click. Then they were alone.

Leesa glanced sideways and saw the cowboy staring at the chair and the tissues too. If she didn't do this now, she feared she'd chicken out. With one hand she pushed him into the seat. He gazed up at her and waited. She had a feeling he'd wait there all night if she made him. She was definitely in charge here.

There was a knob on the wall behind his head. She leaned over and spun it. Music filled the small space and made it seem like they were even further removed from the crowd outside that door. When she pulled back, she saw his eyes focused on her breasts. She couldn't blame him, after all, she was topless and they were in a strip club. He may be shy, but he was definitely all male.

Leesa ran one fingernail slowly down his bare chest, all the way to the fine line of hair showing just above his buckle. If she wasn't mistaken, he'd shivered from the touch. It made her want to see if she could make him react that strongly to all her touches. "What do you want me to do, cowboy?"

She wouldn't have asked that question of just any man, but this guy seemed different somehow. Safer.

He swallowed hard before he spoke. "What are the rules?"

Hmm. Maybe this wasn't his first time in a strip club if he knew there were house rules. "That doesn't matter right now. Tonight, I make the rules."

"Oh." For a second she thought she'd scared him away with her proclamation, until his eyes boldly met hers from beneath the brim of his hat. "What do you want to do?"

She liked his response. Her choice. She was in control. That thought calmed her nerves a bit.

As Leesa felt the persistent warmth that began between her legs and spread throughout her body, she definitely couldn't tell him what she really wanted to do with him. Things couldn't go that far. Not here. Not now. Another time, another place, another lifetime perhaps, maybe it could have happened between her and this sweet guy.

Suppressing that wistful thought, she instead focused on all she could do here and now. "Why don't I just show you?"

He took his hat off and hooked it on the doorknob. After running his hand through his dark blond curls, he nodded. "Okay."

Leesa smiled at how he seemed to brace himself in the chair, as if ready for anything, good or bad. She decided to begin slowly, thinking being gentle with her shy cowboy at first would be the best course of action. Swinging her hips in time with the music, she started by running her fingers over her body, from her bare breasts down to the thin string stretched across her hips.

His gaze followed the motion of her hands, but then

returned to settle on her face. The intensity in his gaze was starting to make Leesa self-conscious. She turned so she could no longer see him watching. She moved backward, closer until she hovered just above him, then she got even closer. She pressed against him, her ass grinding his crotch. His hands, warm and large, moved to rest lightly on her hips.

Normally the customers weren't supposed to touch the girls, not even during a lap dance, but tonight Leesa didn't ask him to remove his hands. Instead, she ground against him harder. His hands slid up to her ribcage. One thumb lightly brushed the side of her breast, sending a tingle through her. Again she could have asked him not to touch her. Again, she didn't.

She could feel the outline of him, hard as steel, pushing into the soft flesh of her butt. How in the world would she go about doing what Holly had told her to do? Did she just open his pants and grab him? Should she tell him to undo the belt and jeans himself? His massively ornate buckle looked like it wouldn't be easy to open. Especially since her hands were shaking.

Entertaining all these errant thoughts still didn't change the fact that she hadn't been this aroused by a man, a stranger no less, in a very long time.

Rotating beneath his grasp, she slowly turned to face him again. She straddled the cowboy in the chair and pressed close. Once more she felt the electricity coursing between them. Her breath caught in her throat.

The sexual chemistry was palpable. He definitely felt it too. Leesa could tell that simply by looking at him. His eyes, heavily lidded with wanting her, focused intensely on her face. His hands grasped her hips tightly. She felt every quickened breath he took, even as her own gasps filled her ears. He pressed her closer, guiding her gyrations against him. His gaze never left hers, as if he was watching for her to react.

If a reaction was what he wanted, he got it. Every movement increased her need and brought her closer to orgasm. Gripping the back of his chair for support as her legs weakened, she leaned forward until her nipples grazed his bare chest. At the contact he let out a sound that seemed half-pleasure, half-pain. He increased the speed of their thrusting and Leesa's body erupted in waves of pleasure.

Eyes closed, she rode the orgasm, and the cowboy, for what felt like forever, but at the same time, not nearly long enough.

She'd just let a customer make her come. Never had that happened before. Never had she wanted it to happen before. If she didn't move off him, he'd likely do it again she was wound so tightly right now.

When she finally opened her eyes and, panting, pulled back enough to look at his face, it was to find he had beads of sweat forming on his smooth upper lip. His erection was still pressed between them. She could only imagine what it felt like for him to be that hard and squashed in tight jeans.

She remembered she was here for his pleasure, not her own. Leesa shifted her position so her now-wobbly legs straddled only one of his thighs. Still recovering from the unexpected climax that had rocked her, she reached down and touched his belt with hands that felt weak. After focusing her brain enough to study how it opened, she fiddled a bit and managed to release the buckle, all as he watched. Luckily it hadn't been as difficult as she'd assumed because she didn't think she had the concentration or the strength to wrestle with it at the moment.

With hands that trembled, she undid the button and zipper on his jeans and pushed the fly open wide. No longer constrained, his erection sprang up, tenting the fabric of his navy blue boxer shorts. She touched it through the thin layer of cotton, raising her gaze to his face as she did.

Breathing heavily, he stared at her hand as it lightly stroked him. When he realized she was watching him, he raised his eyes to stare into hers. His tongue peeked out and nervously licked his lips as he drew in a shaky breath. She continued to watch him as she reached beneath the elastic band and touched the warm, velvety skin covering his rock-hard erection. She stroked him slowly, gently at first. As his breathing quickened, so did her speed until his eyes closed and she felt his body tense beneath her.

He bit his lip as his hand covered hers. She watched with fascination the sight of their hands joined, clasped around him. Squeezing her fist tighter around his length, he moved their hands together. Slow at first, then faster. His breath increased with the speed of their stroking.

Suddenly he released his grasp. He reached down and grabbed a tissue from the box next to the chair. With teeth clenched and eyes slammed tight, she felt his shaft throb in her hand as he came into the tissue.

Now that the deed was done, Leesa wasn't quite sure what to do with herself. He, on the other hand, seemed perfectly comfortable with the situation.

Recovering quickly, he opened his eyes and let out a small laugh. He shook his head as he grabbed more tissues and wiped off his hand. When he'd wadded up the whole mess and pitched it into the corner where it landed in a garbage pail she hadn't noticed before, he turned his attention back to her. Once again she felt the full scrutiny of his intense stare.

"That was—" He shook his head once again, as if at a loss for words. His voice was soft and breathy.

"Yeah, it was." Her own voice came out pretty breathless too. She swallowed hard and realized she was still perched on his leg and he could probably feel the hot wetness not contained by the G-string. She moved to get up but he grabbed her hand and stopped her.

"Wait. Can I see you again?"

"See me?"

See her how? Was he talking about coming back for another hand job tomorrow? Or maybe for more than just a hand job next time. After what she'd done with him, he probably expected she did that and more with all the customers. Why wouldn't he make that assumption?

"Yeah." He nodded. "When do you get done here? Maybe we could meet up afterward for a drink. Or tomorrow. I have a thing I have to be at for a few hours, but I could take you out to lunch, or dinner if you're not working."

She felt her brows rise. "You mean like a date?"

"Yup." He grinned. "I really want to see you again."

Why? For sex, or did he really like her? There was definitely mutual attraction. She felt it too, but he didn't even know her. He knew nothing more than what she'd done with him for the past half hour or so.

Maybe he truly wanted to get to know her. Could he really be as nice as he appeared? It all made her head spin. "Um—"

A knock on the door interrupted her answer, not that she had an answer to his question.

"Hey! Times up. One of the other girls needs the room." The bouncer's voice sounded through the thin door, knocking her back to reality.

She glanced down at the man beneath her and realized his jeans were still wide open and his boxers exposed. "Okay,

Bruno. Give me one minute."

Leesa rose and this time he let her, mostly because his hands were busy dressing himself. She pulled the edges of her vest together and crossed her arms over her bare breasts, suddenly feeling exposed now that the fantasy moment between them had been shattered by real life.

With his shirt buttoned and tucked into his buckled jeans once again, the cowboy stood, hat held in front of him by both hands. "So, about our date..."

Leesa glanced at the door, knowing their time was very limited. That was probably for the best. Where the hell could this thing with him go? She knew the answer to that. Nowhere.

"I'm sorry. I don't date customers." She turned to go when she felt his hand on her elbow. She paused and waited.

"Oh. Okay. Um, then here. This is for you."

Looking back, she saw he held a folded bill in his hand. He thrust it toward her. Her gut took a plunge. She shook her head. "Your friends are paying for the lap dance." The rest, she suddenly didn't want money for.

"I know. They told me they were paying, but this is a tip. From me."

Leesa swallowed hard. She had done it for the extra cash. Hadn't she? Then why didn't she want his money? Because taking it for what she'd done over and above the bought-and-paid-for lap dance made her something she never even imagined she'd become. Even if in another time and another place she probably would have done it with this guy simply because she liked him.

With lids lowered to hide the tears welling in her eyes she grabbed the bill. "Thanks." Then she left the room and him behind her and didn't look back.

She was vaguely aware of one of the new girls working the pole up on stage. She was conscious enough of her surroundings to be relieved she wouldn't have to perform again too soon since the rest of the girls on the shift had finally arrived. Hopefully she could hide until he and his friends had left. She walked straight to the locker room and found Holly there.

Holly's face lit up when she saw her. "Well? How did it go?"

"Fine." She kept her head buried in her locker, pretending she was putting her tips in her purse when really she just needed time to regain her composure.

"His friend gave me the money for your lap dance since you disappeared in back with the birthday boy so quick."

Leesa looked up and took the money Holly offered her. "Thanks."

"Did you, you know, earn any extra while you were there?"

Leesa knew exactly what Holly was asking. "Yeah. I did."

Of course Holly would have yelled at her if she told her she didn't set a price in advance, didn't ask for payment up front, didn't even ask for money she'd been so...what? Wrapped up in enjoying him?

She glanced down at the folded bill. It was a twenty. She felt like laughing and crying at the same time. She'd sold her soul for twenty dollars and because of that, she somehow felt that she'd never ever be the same.

Holly's hand touched her shoulder. "You okay?"

"Yeah." She lied.

"He wasn't an ass or anything, was he? I really thought he looked sweet."

Leesa could hear the concern in Holly's voice. That concern just about did Leesa in. Coupled with the fact that he truly was

39

sweet, the kind of guy she'd probably fall for if she hadn't just serviced him sexually for cash, the tears fell in earnest now.

Still hiding her face, Leesa shook her head. "No, you were right. He was a nice guy. Really. I'm fine. Just tired. I'm going to splash some water on my face and try to wake up before I need to go on again."

"Okay, sweetie. Take your time. Let the latecomers entertain the crowd for a bit, then I'll go up. Take all the time you need."

"Thanks." Leesa slammed her locker door and headed straight for the private, single-stall bathroom next to Jerry's office instead of the public ladies' room out front. His door wasn't closed all the way.

She tiptoed past, not in the mood for him to call her inside and yell at her for bothering him during his meeting before. Through the crack it looked like he was alone now and talking on the phone.

"Yeah, she busted into the office and saw both him and the cash."

She stopped dead in her tracks.

Jerry had kept his voice low when he'd spoken, which was something he rarely did, so it caught her attention and made her listen closer, as did what he was saying. He had to be talking about her. She stepped off to the side of the door, out of sight but within hearing.

"Come on, Johnny. Do you really think that's necessary? She's just a stupid bitch. Who's she gonna tell?"

Leesa swallowed hard. What or rather who had she seen that she wasn't supposed to have? What was bad enough to make Jerry's brother, Johnny, ask him to do something even a lowlife like Jerry didn't want to do?

"No, you're still in charge. I'm just saying, I think knocking her off is a little drastic considering—"

Her stomach lurched. Knocking her off? Was her life in danger just because she'd made a silly error in judgment and walked in on what was obviously some illegal business deal?

"No, I'll take care of it. I'll have Bruno do it after the shift... Come on, man! I have a club to run. If we take her out before the shift's over I'll be short a girl—"

Leesa didn't wait to hear the rest. She backed up as quickly and silently as she could and then, when she was a good distance from his office, she turned and ran. At her locker, she pulled her knee-length jacket on over what was left of her costume, changed her shoes and shoved the rest of her clothes into her oversized purse.

Holly was still there changing for her next number. She stopped lacing up her boots and frowned at Leesa. "What's the matter, hon?"

Panicked, Leesa didn't know what to tell her. She needed to buy some time and save herself, but she also felt like she had to keep Holly out of it and safe. "I can't tell you. Holly, I need you to do something for both me and for you. Okay?"

Frowning, Holly nodded. "Okay."

Leesa glanced nervously back toward Jerry's office. "If anyone—Jerry, Bruno, anyone—asks where I am, tell them I'm in the ladies' room out front. Tell them I have cramps, or I don't know, chronic diarrhea. Something that will keep them from looking for me for a while. All right?"

She couldn't fight the feeling that if she didn't leave now, she might never have the chance.

"All right. It's better if I don't know why, isn't it?" Holly's expression told Leesa she'd been around the seedy side of this world enough to know to stay out of it.

"Yeah, it is."

"Okay, hon. I'll do what I can to give you some time." Holly pulled her into a hug. They both knew this could be the last time they saw each other.

"Thanks. I gotta go." Leesa's panic and fear squelched the tears that surely would have been falling otherwise. Adrenaline was a powerful drug.

Holly released her from the embrace. "Good luck."

And with that Leesa left. For where, she didn't know. Only that it had to be far from here.

Chapter Four

"Hey, man. Time to get up." Those distant words eventually penetrated the hazy, peaceful darkness of sleep.

Chase became aware of something, or rather someone, annoyingly poking him in the arm. Seconds later his brain registered his hangover from hell. It didn't really hit him until he rolled over and felt his stomach rebel. He cracked one lid open and the beam of sunlight hitting him in the eye felt like a knife cutting through his skull.

"Ugh. What time is it?"

"It's just after noon." Garret supplied the answer in a voice that sounded far too chipper considering Chase's current state.

He winced at the horrid taste in his mouth and considered if drinking some water would make him feel better or worse. With his brain working in slow motion, it took Chase a moment to process fully what Garret had told him. "Noon? I never sleep this late."

Fully dressed and looking ready for a bright new day, Garret grinned at Chase without one ounce of sympathy. "You also usually don't roll back to our room wasted at four thirty in the morning and then proceed to do shots of tequila."

"I did shots?" And if so, he would never have done them alone. Why the hell did Garret seem so awake when Chase felt like death warmed over?

Leaning against the dresser across the room, arms crossed, Garret nodded. "Oh yeah, you did. But what I find most interesting is that as drunk as you were, you still wouldn't tell me what went on with you and that stripper in the back room."

The memory of the events from the night before cut through the fog clouding his brain. Not only did all that had happened in the back room clearly fill his hazy mind, so did a sudden realization.

Chase's suspicions rose even if his body hadn't quite been able to do so yet. The reason Garret wasn't hung over was suddenly clear to Chase. "Did you stay sober last night and get me drunk just to get information out of me?"

Garret grinned. "Oh, come on. Would I do that?"

"Yes." Chase sat up and immediately regretted it as what felt like a lightning bolt pierced his skull. He pressed one hand to his stomach as it gave an angry lurch. "I could kill you. I feel like shit and we have that fan thing in like two hours."

As painful as it was, he still managed to shoot Garret a nasty look.

"It's your own fault. If you would've just told me what happened with the hottie in the back room, I wouldn't have had to ply you with alcohol. And FYI, I am so trusting you with all of my secrets from now on, because you, man, are like a vault. You never cracked. Not even once. You threw up, but you never spilled the beans."

He'd thrown up? That explained the foul taste in his mouth.

"If I were you, I wouldn't trust me at all. In fact, you better consider not falling asleep tonight because I'm serious about killing you for this." As soon as he could stand without falling over or throwing up again, Chase intended to get right on that.

Garret dismissed his threat with the casual wave of one

hand. "Yeah, yeah. Whatever. You stink like tequila. Go shower so we can get something to eat before the fan thing. I'm starving."

The thought of food sent Chase's stomach reeling, but a nice hot shower might help. He rose gingerly, as if his head was made of glass and any sudden movements might break it. At this point, that was pretty much exactly what it felt like as Chase made his way across the room to the bathroom, which seemed a longer distance than it had yesterday.

"Oh, and I forgot to tell you. The guys wanna do something good tonight."

Chase frowned. "Wasn't last night good enough for you?"

"Well, yeah, but tonight is our last night here so we have to do something fun, but everyone's bitching about how much money we've spent this week. The plan is we're staying in and having a party right here."

"Fine. Whatever." Chase shuffled through the bathroom doorway, not caring what anybody did as long as they left him alone now.

Garret called after him. "We'll pick up some beer or whatever after the meet-and-greet."

"Great. Can't wait." Chase smothered a moan at the thought.

As he closed the bathroom door, he heard Garret laugh. "You'll recover."

"Yeah, I know." The sooner the better, so he could get to killing Garret.

The hot spray of water helped immensely, as did the time alone to think. Once he decided he wasn't going to hurl, Chase started to recount the events of the night before. At least the parts he could remember. The events before Garret started pouring drinks down his throat.

Images of the strip club filled his tequila-soaked brain. He didn't even know her name, but he could still see her face as clearly as if she was there in front of him. Chase could almost feel her touch on him too.

Damn. Why hadn't he asked her name? Not that it would have made much difference since she said she didn't date customers. But what if he wasn't a customer? What if he never went back to the club again? Then could he ask her out? Tonight was their last night in town, at least until next season when the tour came back this way again. Would she even still be working there next year so he could find her?

The reality was, there was no way he wanted to wait that long to find out anyway, and not just because of what had happened between them either. Okay, yeah. That had been pretty freaking amazing, but it was more. He liked what he saw in her eyes, though he could never tell Garret or any of the other guys that. They didn't get it. They made fun of him enough as it was. Calling him Romeo. Telling him he got attached too easily.

Sure he could tell them about the hand job and they'd slap him on the back and congratulate him, but he couldn't say anything about how he felt about it. How there was far more passing between them than just a happy-ending lap dance. The moment he mentioned asking her out because he wanted to get to know her better as a person, they'd do nothing but tease him.

So he liked getting to know the women he was with better, while his friends were happy with one-night-stands. So what? Maybe he selected his women more carefully to begin with. He was drawn to those who were worth getting attached to, instead of just hooking up with for one night. What was wrong with that? Nothing, as far as he could see.

Yeah, he'd only known her for maybe an hour, but he liked her. There was substance there. He saw something deep down. Stuff she tried to hide from the world, but he saw it. He was good at reading people. He always had been. She had struck Chase as strong but vulnerable underneath. She was bold but scared at the same time.

He'd felt her trembling, and not just from what he suspected—or at least hoped—was her orgasm during that lap dance. Not that he'd been to a hell of a lot of those kinds of places, but the guys had dragged him into a few strip clubs in their travels. They usually ended up at one whenever someone was getting married or had a birthday. Over the years, Chase had had contact with enough strippers to know they didn't usually blush, or get so nervous with a customer they started shaking.

As he soaped himself inside the steamy stall and thought about her, he realized he felt a little better. One part of him was recovering exceptionally fast. Chase considered ignoring it, then thought what the hell. He couldn't come up with a better way to wake up and get ready for the day.

Wishing he had a name to go with the vision of her face and the rest of his really nice memories of their time together, Chase grabbed himself and started stroking. He knew immediately it wasn't going to take long. Not with the tantalizing images of her filling his brain. Even while she was somewhere else the woman did it for him. He quickly came into the hot stream of water.

The first thought to hit him afterward was that perhaps he would be able to eat after all. Some food and a few ibuprofen and he'd be good as new.

Somehow they'd found her. How?

She'd been careful. Leesa had only allowed herself perhaps ten minutes to stop home. Barely long enough to fling the few things she needed, or couldn't live without, into a bag. Her entire life fit into an oversized tote bag. How sad was that? She reminded herself that at least she still had a life. For now anyway. That could change in an instant if she didn't keep on her toes and get the hell out of town unnoticed and soon.

No one had followed her car when she'd left her apartment. She was certain, or at least so she had thought. She'd headed to the casino where she knew she would find enough people to hide her for a few hours until she could grab one of the buses heading out of town.

She'd ditched her vehicle in the casino's covered parking lot amid thousands of others knowing Jerry and Johnny must have dirty cops on their payroll who could have tracked the car registered to her if she'd driven it out of town. She thought no one would notice it parked here. Apparently she'd been wrong because the undeniable fact remained they were here and because of that she wasn't safe. She had to get out, but where would she go?

Heart pounding, she considered that question. Meanwhile, Bruno, wearing his usual black T-shirt and slacks, and two gorillas dressed in what looked like thousand-dollar Italian suits with shoulder-holster bulges the size of her forearm were headed in her direction. Their very presence proved they somehow knew she was here in the casino, but judging by the way they moved—slowly, visually searching the room—they hadn't spotted her yet.

She turned and headed in the opposite direction, all the while fighting the urge to look over her shoulder. Her pulse sounded so loudly in her ears, she had to strain to listen over its pounding. Above the background din of the crowd, she prayed she wouldn't hear the bouncer's familiar voice call her name as they closed in on her. She walked quickly but not so fast it would attract their attention. Blending in, being able to disappear amid these people, might possibly be a matter of life and death.

The problem was as a young woman she didn't blend very well with the senior citizens perched on stools at the slot machines that surrounded her now. There was nowhere to get truly lost in this particular area. She needed a thicker, more diverse crowd. Leaning against a tall slot machine, she paused to catch her breath and think. Panicking wouldn't help. She had to be rational. She needed a plan.

The air conditioning pumped out icy cold air, probably to keep the gamblers awake and at their machines, but Leesa could feel the cold sweat of fear on her skin. If she lowered her head toward her chest, she could even smell the fear radiating off her, or maybe it was simply that she hadn't showered since yesterday. She'd spent the last twelve hours or so in the casino, moving constantly. Waiting to escape. Thinking Jerry would assume she'd immediately left town and not be looking for her to be on a later bus. She had obviously been wrong. She'd waited too long.

Leesa wished she'd had the money for a plane ticket, though they'd probably be watching the airport too.

An amplified announcement followed by the sound of cheering broke through the steady drone of slots and conversation. Leesa glanced up and could have cried with relief at what she saw. It was relief, or maybe hunger and exhaustion, that had her on the verge of tears. Either way, it didn't matter because now she had a plan.

Farther down the shop-lined hall leading away from the

age-restricted, railed-in area filled with slot machines and gamblers, a very large, noisy crowd clustered. A closer look proved it was made up of young and old, men, women and children. She had no idea why they were here, but the more people to get lost among the better. Head down, she made a beeline to that diverse group of strangers who may just unknowingly save her.

Sliding into the tight space between a jean-clad man in cowboy boots and a girl wearing a tight, belly-baring T-shirt and jeans cut low enough to show her thong, Leesa hoped to hide in the crowd. She glanced down at her own sweatshirt and jeans, her pitiful attempt to become invisible. She prayed it would work.

Life was pretty surreal at the moment, kind of like a strange, horrifying nightmare she couldn't wake up from, but the man in full clown makeup and wearing a cowboy hat while addressing the gatherers through a microphone attached to his head made things seem even stranger. He called out a steady stream of banter while shooting T-shirts and hats with a handheld rocket launcher into the midst of the slightly unruly group. She didn't know what was happening around her or why, but if it helped her avoid being caught, she'd take the good fortune without question.

Another blast was followed by shouts from the assembled masses. The tall man next to her extended an arm and caught one of the bundles the clown shot at them. He held the prize down to her.

"Do you want this? I have three already." He grinned wide, showing a wad of chewing tobacco shoved into his cheek.

"Thanks." Nodding, she reached for it, too surprised by the offer and traumatized by the current state of her world to do anything else.

A hat wasn't a bad idea. One glance around proved more than a few others were wearing their clown-propelled baseball hats already.

Maybe she'd duck into the restroom and change into the T-shirt later too. Should she hide in the ladies' room until the coast was clear? The thought of being trapped in a relatively small, windowless space with only one way out, that being the exit that could be blocked by the goons, left her with an even sicker feeling in her gut than she'd had when she'd first spotted them. No, out here among lots of witnesses felt safer. Or at least as safe as she was going to get for now.

It didn't take long to unwrap the tie holding the hat and shirt together. With a hand she noticed was shaking, she brushed her hair back from her face and pulled the baseball cap over it. She should have thought to buy scissors and hair dye. They'd be looking for her with long, brown hair. Then again, she'd never thought they'd get this close to finding her in the first place, so how could she have predicted she'd need to change her appearance? The plan to drive to the casino, abandon her car and then hop on one of the many busses leaving from there each afternoon for all parts of the country should have worked.

Why didn't it? How the hell had they found her? She still didn't know, but for now the hat would do to hide her until she could figure things out.

She pulled the cap lower over her eyes and positioned herself behind the bulk of the man next to her. Only then did she dare to turn and look for her pursuers.

It didn't take long to spot them. As they moved in her direction, their beady eyes swept the space in a practiced move. Her simple disguise wasn't going to work if they spotted her. She needed to move.

The cell phone in her front pocket vibrated against her hip. She jumped and stifled a small cry. Then realization hit her. Could Jerry trace her location from her cell phone being on even if she didn't answer it?

Of course he could. She should have thought of that before. Jerry's brother, Johnny, was reputed to be some big shit with mob connections. He was powerful enough he could do anything he wanted and no one would question him. His umbrella of influence even extended to Jerry. Everyone simply said yes to both brothers. People jumped to please them, even the cops, which is why she was totally on her own.

But she wouldn't be alone for much longer if she didn't ditch her phone. She'd have three very mean men for unwanted company.

A family walked toward her as she frantically tried to plan. Should she take out the cell phone's battery? Would that help? As Leesa's panic dulled her ability to think, the woman pushed a baby carriage with a sleepy-looking child inside past her, while the man walked by holding a toddler in his arms. Bits of conversation reached Leesa's ears as they passed her.

The man spoke. "I'll take him to the men's room with me and then we'll leave?"

The woman nodded. "Yeah, she's not going to fall asleep here. Maybe she will in the car."

Forcing herself to move slowly, calmly, she slipped to the edge of the crowd while still remaining hidden by the bodies around her. She slid the phone out of her pocket and with trembling fingers adjusted the mode to totally silent instead of vibrate. The father disappeared into the bathroom while the mother moved in front of the stroller, her attention totally consumed in trying to get the baby to stop fussing.

As casually as she could muster given the pounding of her

heart, Leesa let her phone drop into the diaper bag hanging from the stroller's handles. With any luck they wouldn't notice the small cell phone stowing away in their bag right away. Instead, they would take Jerry's search for her on a wild goose chase to some hopefully far away suburb.

She stifled the feeling of guilt that she might bring harm to an innocent family by using them to get away. Then again, Jerry and his brother had nothing against these people. It was her they wanted, even though why was still a mystery. Who or what had Leesa seen that could cost her life? She couldn't think about that now.

The crowd sheltering her started moving toward a set of doors. They formed somewhat orderly lines at each of the many entrances leading into another area. Looking around, she noticed everyone clutched tickets in their hand. Each doorway was blocked by similarly dressed men who she assumed were stationed there to collect those tickets.

Leesa would have to move with the crowd or be exposed again but she didn't have a ticket. Her heart rate sped faster with panic.

A woman pulled a child by the hand toward the restrooms. "Why didn't you say you had to go to the bathroom before? Now we're gonna miss getting a good spot in line for the autographs."

During the dragging, the contrite-looking boy dropped the ticket he'd been holding. Neither mother nor child noticed as the small white paper drifted and came to rest just feet from Leesa. While they kept going and disappeared into the bathroom, the lost ticket remained on the floor.

Smothering any guilt she felt for basically stealing from a child, Leesa bent and scooped up the paper. Hiding it in the palm of her hand, she glanced at the printing on it.

There was a logo of some sort, and the words *Fan Meet and*

Greet. It listed today's date. Not sure who she'd be meeting or greeting, she took her place among the line that funneled people slowly through a door into what looked to be a restricted area separate from the main part of the casino. Hopefully there would be a back emergency exit out of the room, just in case she needed it. In any case, following the crowd into this private event was preferable to being out in the open and exposed to the bad guys advancing in her direction.

A man in a large black cowboy hat checked her ticket and then motioned her inside. Here she'd be hidden from view of anyone without a ticket, such as the guys looking for her. They'd be stuck outside in the hall because somehow she didn't think the tough-looking cowboys with the heavy drawls manning the entrances were under Jerry's brother's sphere of influence.

Leesa drew in a shaky breath of relief and felt moderately safer, for now. She'd won this round, but round two was still ahead. She still had to get away from here and from them. To where, she had no clue. Going home was not an option. She couldn't put her parents in danger.

She was truly alone.

Chapter Five

Chase pulled the metal chair from beneath the table with a loud scrape and sat heavily. His hangover was manageable now that he'd eaten, but he still felt like he could easily lie down and sleep for the rest of the day. Maybe even through to tomorrow when he would start the drive for Oklahoma and home.

Garret plopped down into the folding chair next to him. They were seated near the back of the room filled with forty bull riders, all lined up on one side of a long row of tables.

"You know, when we're done with this thing, you're telling me exactly what happened in that back room." Garret grabbed the marker from the table and sat armed and ready for the onslaught of fans as the doors were opened and people of all ages, shapes and sizes began to filter in.

"Why are you still harping on this?" Chase picked up his own marker and waited too, hoping the smell of tequila wasn't still seeping out of his sweat glands and pores. He was a role model for the younger fans, after all. He couldn't smell like he'd just scraped himself off a barroom floor. "I told you, Garret. Nothing happened."

"Something damn well better have happened. I paid for it to. I seriously hope you got a good lap dance at least."

"Will you please hush up? They're letting the fans in." At Garret's deep frown, Chase decided he'd better appease him with something before Garret stormed back into the club and demanded a refund. Visions of what had really happened filled Chase's head. He'd gotten the lap dance, all right, plus some, but he wasn't going to tell anyone that. "Don't worry. You got your money's worth. Okay?"

Garret seemed pleased by that revelation. "Good, but actually it was you who got my money's worth. Though I didn't do too badly with that other dancer myself. She gave me one hell of a lap dance right at our table. We didn't get to go into the private back room the way you did for a little extra—"

Chase kicked his friend under the table none too gently with the toe of his boot.

"Shh. Garret, people can hear you." He glanced up at the elderly woman approaching the bull rider at the table next to his. Hopefully, she had poor hearing.

Garret sighed. "Damn. I hope this thing doesn't go too late. I can barely keep my eyes open."

Eying a table in the corner covered in canned soft drinks, Chase regretted not grabbing one before he sat down. Caffeine sounded pretty good right about now. Yeah, he'd slept until noon, but he wasn't sure passing out drunk just before sunrise was the equivalent of getting a good night's sleep.

A nap sounded pretty good, but Chase doubted he'd be able to sleep if he went upstairs and laid down after this thing anyway. He kept reliving over and over again every detail of what had happened, even now, out in public. He only imagined it would be worse alone in bed. Being tired was a small price to pay for the incredible memories from last night. He wouldn't have changed a thing.

He smothered a big yawn that snuck out of him.

"Dude, you better rally." Garret's voice held a tinge of panic. "Aaron's brother is going out while we're here and is picking up beer and bourbon for us. I'm hoping to find a couple of hot chicks at this thing to invite up to our floor for the party after."

Chase laughed. "Relax. I'll be okay once I get something to drink."

"I hear ya. A little hair of the dog that bit you always helps." Garret grinned. "I'd stick to beer though. You don't do too good with the hard stuff."

Chase usually didn't drink the hard stuff. Last night was Garret's doing. "I was talking about drinking a pop for some caffeine, but yeah, I'll be sticking to beer later."

If he could bring himself to drink alcohol at all.

A fan approached Chase's table and Garret's chatter about alcohol thankfully came to an end. For the next hour or two it would be all smiles and autographs and every bull rider on his best behavior. There'd be a few photos and lots of small talk, which was pretty much the same no matter what city they were in. Not that Chase minded at all. Without the fans the sport wouldn't be anything except a bunch of guys watching each other get thrown in the dirt.

It would have been better if the meet and greet wasn't after a night of debauchery however. That wasn't the fans fault though. Come to think of it, it wasn't Chase's fault either. He sent another nasty look at Garret.

In between signing programs and T-shirts, he vowed to come up with a plan for revenge. Chase was just wondering what he could do to get back at his friend when he felt Garret's boot knock into his. He moved his foot, figuring it was an accident, when it happened again.

As he handed a signed T-shirt back to one fan and accepted an event program to sign for the next he shot Garret a sideways glance. "Dude. Why do you keep kicking me?"

When no answer immediately followed, Chase handed the autographed program back to the older woman and her husband, then turned his attention to Garret.

"Check her out." Garret tilted his head toward a woman a few people behind the couple Chase had just finished with. "She's totally your kinda girl."

Garret was matchmaking even as he smiled for a fan and signed his name on a T-shirt for her.

"What?" Chase frowned. What the hell was Garret talking about?

"That chick. Invite her to the party tonight. She looks like your type."

Curious now as to what Garret thought was his type, Chase couldn't help but take a look. Her baseball hat was pulled down low over her eyes. He couldn't see much of her face beneath the brim, and she was still pretty far away, but he saw enough to determine she was cute.

Strangely there was no smile on her face and none of the usual fan interaction. She simply moved from one rider to the next until she was standing in front of the guy seated next to Chase. She silently thrust her program at the Brazilian bull rider. The hair the cap didn't cover was long and a silky brown, just like he liked it. It swung across her shoulders as her head swiveled and she glanced toward the doors.

She turned back to take the program handed to her and then took a step to the side until she was at Chase's table. With him sitting and her standing directly in front of him, he could now see beneath the brim of her hat. He saw her green eyes open wide as she recognized him. It was just about the same moment he recognized her.

He tempered his outward reaction, mainly to prevent Garret from noticing who she was. Dressed down in jeans and a sweatshirt with no makeup, and away from the strip club, it was a good possibility none of the other guys would connect her to last night. He wanted to keep it that way. Chase didn't react on the outside, but inside he reacted in a big way. His pulse began to race and his mouth went dry. That didn't prevent him from doing the one thing he regretted not doing the night before though.

Reaching for her program, Chase asked, "What's your name? Who should I sign this to?"

With sweaty palms, he waited for her answer, hoping she didn't say something like, oh sign in for my father, Bob. He should have worded the question better.

Had she come to see him specifically? Did one of the guys tell her last night who they were and where they'd be today? A dozen questions raced through his head, but for now he'd settle for the answer to just one. Her name.

For some reason, she appeared as nervous as he felt. He watched the tip of her tongue shoot out. He couldn't help picturing that tongue elsewhere, licking something else. Something on him. Something that was beginning to wake up.

She hesitated. "It's Leesa, spelled L-E-E-S-A."

Her voice cut a path right through him. If there had been any doubt in his mind as to who she was before, it was erased when he heard her speak. Memories of that voice against his ear not much more than twelve hours before caused a visceral reaction and he felt himself stiffen even more inside his jeans.

Chase swallowed away the dryness being near her again seemed to cause in his throat. He hadn't felt this nervous around a woman in a long time. "That's a really nice name. I'm Chase. Chase Reese."

"Nice to meet you, Chase."

Nice to meet you?

He frowned. She was definitely trying to act like they didn't know each other. Why? She spoke in a level tone that held no recognition, but she didn't control the look in her eyes as well as she did her voice. She remembered him.

She watched him closely, until she glanced at the doors one more time.

That brought up yet another question. Why was she acting so nervous? Who did she keep checking the entrance for? Did she have a boyfriend? Maybe she didn't want him to see her with a customer she'd been pretty intimate with the night before? Or maybe she didn't want her boss or coworkers to see her. Maybe not dating the customers was a club rule, not her own.

If that was the case, why was she here in the first place? Maybe she simply couldn't stay away from him, just like how he couldn't keep his mind off her. Whatever was happening, he didn't intend to let her get away again, though he wasn't quite sure how to keep her around.

Garret's boot knocked his again. Chase was ready to clock him, until his friend whispered, "Invite her to the party."

The fans intent on getting Chase's signature started to cluster behind Leesa. Others stepped around her and moved on to Garret and then on to the next table. Meanwhile, he had yet to sign her program. He had a horrible feeling once he did and handed it back to her, she'd be gone from his life again. He didn't want that to happen. That kicked him into gear and overrode any shyness or doubt he harbored.

He scribbled her name, something to the effect of *thanks for being a fan* and then his name on the program, then glanced up. "Um, we—the other guys and I—are having a kind of party upstairs right after this is done. Nothing special. Just some beer and chips and stuff, but with all of us staying here, we have the entire floor to ourselves so it should be pretty cool. You know, if you wanted to come." He found himself holding his breath waiting for an answer. "Do you want to?"

She glanced around the room. "When is this over?"

His heart fluttered with excitement that she was even considering it enough to ask. "The meet and greets usually last about an hour or so."

"Then after we could go upstairs together? To your room?"

His heart fluttered with anticipation. "Um, yeah. When I'm finished, we can go upstairs together."

Did she sound excited to be going upstairs with him or was it wishful thinking on his part? Actually, she sounded a little cautious, but that was fine. A woman should be cautious when getting invited somewhere by a guy she barely knew.

Leesa hesitated a beat before asking, "Can I wait in here for you until you're done?"

Out of the corner of his eye, Chase saw Garret watching the discussion with a little too much interest, but he ignored him. "Sure. You can wait right over by the refreshments, if you want. No one will bother you."

"Okay. Thanks." She reached out and took the program he'd autographed but hadn't had the mental capacity to remember to hand back to her. Bypassing the rest of the riders, she went directly to the refreshment table and busied herself with choosing a soft drink.

"Oh my God. How did you do that?" Garret's voice was low and filled with shock.

"Do what? I don't know what you're talking about." Chase glanced at Garret and then took the next program from the fan who'd stepped in front of him the moment Leesa had left. He smiled and pretended Garret wasn't there. "Who should I make this out to?"

"You know exactly *what*," Garret continued to harass Chase even though he should be paying attention to the fan in front of him.

"Here you go. Thanks for coming." Chase returned the signed program to the little boy standing shyly at his table, then dealt with Garret, hoping he'd shut up. "We'll discuss this later. Okay?"

"Fine." Garret released a loud expulsion of breath.

Chase caught him shaking his head and staring in the direction of the refreshment table. He followed the path of Garret's gaze and saw Leesa still there. He felt relief that she appeared really to be waiting for him to finish. For a moment he'd feared she wouldn't.

He saw Leesa tear into a bag of pretzels as if she hadn't eaten in days, all while her gaze kept sweeping the room, in particular the entrances. There was definitely something strange going on, but at least now she was coming upstairs with him. He'd figure it—and her—out eventually. He didn't intend to leave Vegas until he did.

A woman began holding a long conversation with the rider next to him, in Portuguese no less, and caused a lull in the procession of fans to Chase's table. As the rest of the fans waited behind her, Chase used the break to estimate how many more people there were in line and how soon he could get the hell out of there and upstairs with Leesa.

During his perusal of the crowd, he spied a girl with plenty of boobs and skin showing. Leesa may be his type, and he was still amazed Garret had nailed that one on the head, but this chick was definitely Garret's type. This time, it was Chase who did the prodding.

He elbowed Garret and nodded toward the girl in line. "Hey.

Let's invite her upstairs."

"Why? You need two women all for yourself?" Garret scowled.

"Not for me. For you, silly." Chase wanted Garret occupied so he'd stay out of his and Leesa's hair. Hopefully out of their shared room too, if he could manage it. Maybe he could get them to hang in Skeeter's room. Or out in the hallway. Chase didn't care, as long as he had some time with Leesa to talk. Okay, talk and maybe a few other things too.

Garret looked moderately happier at the thought of having this girl for himself. "Okay. Cool. I'll invite her though. You keep your mouth shut on this one, Romeo."

Fine with him. Chase nodded. "No problem."

Glancing one more time and seeing Leesa still there loitering in the corner by the refreshments, Chase couldn't help but smile. Tonight had the potential to be a very good night.

Chapter Six

"Ready to go upstairs?" The cowboy had snuck up on her.

She hadn't noticed him while she was staring at the door. She needed to make sure Bruno and company hadn't wiggled their way inside without a ticket, or hadn't somehow bought or perhaps procured a ticket by less-than-honorable means the way she had.

Chase's eyes crinkled with the smile he sent in her direction. The same smile she'd seen last night when he'd asked her out just moments after cleaning himself up after what she'd done with him. Seeing him here was a really strange coincidence. One that was working in her favor so she accepted it gladly.

Leesa had discovered during her time in Vegas, that for a huge city, it could be a very small world. Her running into the same guy she'd danced for was a bit of a long shot, yes, but things like that had happened to her before. At least this was not an unpleasant coincidence. Of all the men she met at the club nightly, this guy was probably the one she'd be most likely to trust to help her, no questions asked. No quid pro quo either. He may hope for a repeat of last night, but he wouldn't force it on her. She'd felt that vibe from him at the club. He was a man, and yes, he was interested, but he was also a gentleman and would respect the word no...if she could bring herself to tell him no. The way he'd made her feel, she wasn't so sure she was capable of saying the word.

What was strange was she wasn't exactly sure if he recognized her or not. She was dressed differently enough there was no reason for him to make the connection. She'd thought she'd seen a flash of recognition in his face, but he didn't say anything or act like he remembered her from last night. He did invite her upstairs, but she wasn't sure he wouldn't have invited a total stranger. Leesa had noticed a few other cowboys talking to girls who it appeared they'd just met, and some of them were likely going up to this party too. Cowboys were apparently popular with the ladies.

Was her sweet innocent cowboy really a player? Glancing at him again, she realized if he was she'd have to deal with it all later. Right now it was most important she get out of the public area before she was spotted.

Forcing a smile, she nodded in response to his last question. "I'm ready."

Her answer was met by an even wider grin that showed his strong, white teeth. This guy could be the poster boy for good, clean country living.

"Good." Cutie that he was, he grabbed her hand and laced his fingers through hers, like they were middle-schoolers on their first date. She had to admit she liked it. His strong hand holding hers made her feel safe, but the direction he was leading them didn't. As he pulled her toward the main doors, she planted her sneakers firmly and tugged against his grasp.

He stopped. "Did you forget something?"

"Um, no. It's just there are so many people outside. Maybe we can leave through a back door?" She had already scoped out all the back exits.

Apparently Chase and these other guys were some sort of

celebrities, though she wasn't sure what kind. People had lined up to get Chase's autograph, so maybe he'd be convinced to avoid a fan mob scene out in the hallway.

He paused and glanced at the entrance. Luckily there was a small group of people milling around out there. "I guess a few people didn't get tickets. Sure. We can head out the back if you want. Though the way I've been riding most of this year, I'm not sure I'd be the one the fans would be hanging around waiting for."

She nodded, not understanding his self-deprecating grin or why how he rode would dictate how many fans waited for him. Come to think of it, she wasn't sure what he rode either. It must be horses, she guessed. Cowboys ride horses. Right?

It didn't matter. Leesa was simply relieved they'd be going out the back way where she'd be less likely to be killed by Bruno and his hit squad.

Chase paused, settling his gaze on the bag hanging on her shoulder whose weight had her listing slightly to the left. "Do you want me to carry that for you? It looks pretty heavy."

"Um, no. That's okay. It's not that heavy." *Shit.* She'd have to explain the giant bag she was toting around. "I'm, uh, on my way out of town for a little vacation. I was just killing some time in the casino before my bus leaves."

Killing some time. Trying not to get killed. Whatever.

"What time is that?"

His question took her by surprise. She was a horrid liar. "What?"

"Your bus. When do you have to leave?"

"Oh, I uh hadn't made exact plans. I was just going to hop on a bus whenever I felt like it."

He grinned wide. "A free spirit, huh?"

Leesa shrugged. "Yup, that's me. I go wherever the wind blows me."

He had no idea how funny that idea was. He should have seen her with her nose in a book studying twenty-four-seven back in college. She used to have every moment of every day scheduled and timed, right down to her meals and when she'd shower. Things had sure changed.

"I'm glad about that." His smile that reached all the way to his eyes told her he truly was.

"Why?" Damn, she could really like this guy.

"Because maybe you being a free spirit means you'll stick around for a bit." In spite of Chase's ever-present grin and good mood, he still seemed to search right down to her very soul when he stared deeply into her eyes.

Leesa swallowed hard. "Maybe."

For what felt like a ridiculously long time, another one of those *moments* passed between them. It didn't matter the room was full of strangers and noise. Just like it had happened on stage at the club, it felt as if they were the only two people in the world.

She shook off the feeling. "Shall we go upstairs?"

"Sure."

The look on Chase's face could only be categorized as gleeful. Then her hand was squeezed by his and she was being pulled toward the back door. She held her breath with fear as Chase reached out and pushed the door wide, then, gentleman that he was, waited for her to walk through first.

Peering into the hallway, left and then right, she looked for the faces she dreaded seeing. She pulled the hat a little lower over her forehead. Seeing the coast was clear for now, she asked, "Which way to the elevator?"

Chase tilted his head to the right. "It's just up here a ways."

Leesa nodded, hoping *just up here a ways* in cowboy-speak meant closer rather than farther.

Soon, she thought. Soon they'd be upstairs in Chase's room on a floor he'd said would be entirely filled with his fellow cowboys, and Bruno and his killer friends wouldn't be able to find her. Besides, by now they should be following the cell phone in the poor unsuspecting family's diaper bag.

Every step of her feet against the floor of the hall seemed to echo off the walls and through her head, like a metronome ticking off the time. Time she knew she didn't have. Time she couldn't waste if she wanted to survive. Then Leesa heard the familiar and oh-so-welcome ding that heralded an elevator nearby. She nearly cried at the sound.

Chase's hand squeezed hers tightly as they stood in front of the closed brass doors. He pushed the button and smiled down at her. Eventually she'd have to deal with the way her heart fluttered every time she looked at him. Worse, how strongly her body reacted when he looked at her. She'd also have to figure out if he recognized her or not. But for now, just watching the elevator's door slide open made her happy. Chase motioned for her to step inside before he followed one small step behind her.

He pushed the button for his floor. It was one of the higher numbers. She tried not to panic. If she needed to escape down the stairs it would take her a while, longer with each level the elevator rose above ground. Would she ever feel safe again? Probably not. Even if she got away, she'd always be looking over her shoulder, wondering when they'd catch up to her. Not even knowing why they wanted her dead.

Leesa must have let out a sigh without realizing it. When she glanced up, Chase was looking at her with an expression of concern on his face. "You okay?"

She conjured a smile. "Yeah. Fine."

He nodded, though he didn't look totally convinced with her answer. Then the doors opened and the sudden noise and commotion pushed all else out of her mind. Leesa certainly hoped Chase's friends occupied the entire floor because it was looking more like a frat party than a hotel at the moment, right down to the keg sitting in a large bucket filled with ice.

Chase didn't let go of her hand, which she was grateful for, but he did practically drag her out of the elevator with a muttered, "What the hell?"

He stopped in front of the guy Leesa recognized as both the cowboy who'd been seated next to him today at the table, and last night in the club.

"Jeez, Garret. You said Aaron's brother picked up some beer, not a keg. Don't you think we're pushing it a little?"

The guy Chase had called Garret shrugged. "What can they do? Throw us out?"

"Um, yeah. Actually they can." Chase's body tensed next to her. When he looked down at her again, it wasn't with his usual smile.

She wasn't so happy herself. If they got kicked out of here, then what would she do? She'd be right back where she'd been an hour ago. Maybe she could hop on a bus like she'd planned, but if Jerry and his brother had half a brain they would be watching all the buses leaving since they knew she'd been here.

A kid who looked barely out of high school came up to them, big red plastic cup in his hand. He took a big swallow of beer and then glanced from Chase to Garret. "What's wrong with you two?"

"Ah, jeez. I forgot Skeeter's not even old enough to drink. Do you know how much trouble we can get into for serving a minor?" Chase ran his free hand over his face.

Garret shook his head. "Okay, okay. Relax. I hear ya. I don't know when you became such a stick in the mud, but I'll handle it. Skeeter, you and the guys move the keg into my room."

"Uh, no. Move it into one of the other rooms." Chase glanced down at her then back to Garret.

Leesa noted Garret's brows shoot up. He donned a cocky grin and nodded slowly. "Oh. All right. I get it."

As Garret's gaze moved to her, Chase shook his head. "Shut up, Garret."

"What?" Garret's wide-eyed innocence was too animated to be real. "I didn't say anything."

The snort Chase released told what he thought about that answer.

Maybe they both did recognize her from the club. And after what she'd done with him, perhaps they assumed Chase would be getting busy with her in that room. God, maybe they thought she'd service them all for the right price. Was that why they'd brought her up here?

She'd done this to herself by agreeing to do what she'd done last night for cash. Leesa shouldn't care what Garret or anyone else thought of her. The reality was, she couldn't care right now. She had to keep herself safe. She wondered what she'd have to do in order to keep herself that way.

"Come on." Chase pulled her off to one of the rooms farther down the hall. She wasn't so keen on getting there any longer. Chase was more in tune to her emotions than she imagined. He stopped mid-step.

"I'm sorry about Garret. He's just an idiot. I usually ignore most of what he says." When she only nodded but didn't say anything, he continued. "Those guys are going to be drinking that keg until tomorrow morning. I for one was hoping to get to

70

bed before sunrise since I have a bit of a drive to make tomorrow."

"Yeah, good plan." Once the fear and adrenaline left her body, there was a good chance she'd fall asleep standing up. God, she would love to get some sleep in the safety of Chase's room tonight. She'd give anything for that luxury actually.

Chase stuck a keycard in the door. "You can put your bag here in my room where it'll be safe. That way you won't have to tote it around on your shoulder all night."

Leesa kind of wanted to tote it around. Her entire life, what pitiful amount was left of it, was in that bag. Granted, it amounted to a toothbrush and deodorant, a few changes of clothes and a tattered wallet that housed all her money in the world since she'd emptied out her account at an ATM machine on her way to the casino.

There was also an old photo of her family. One of those you got taken at the mall during some holiday or another, when you all dressed alike in matching, usually obnoxiously colored sweaters. Hard to believe her life had gone from that to this—running for her life in Vegas with nothing but the clothes she could carry.

She glanced up to find Chase watching her again. "Um, thanks for inviting me to the party."

Chase let out another derisive snort. "Party. Yeah. I'm sorry I didn't know it was going to be a kegger when I asked you. The guys can get a little out of hand sometimes."

She shrugged. "It's okay. I remember what it was like in college. That's what kids get like when you put them together."

He laughed and shook his head. "Kids."

"What?"

"You're not so old yourself." He swung the door wide and

after sticking his hand in to flip on the light switch on the wall, waited for her to enter before he followed her inside.

"I'm way older than that—what did you call him—Skeeter? Where'd he get a name like that anyway?"

Chase laughed outright now. "I'll let him tell you."

Amazingly, she felt herself smile. "I look forward to it."

The door swung closed behind them with a decisive click, and Leesa felt a new sense of anxiety from being totally alone with Chase again. Almost nervous, like she wanted something to happen, but at the same time was afraid it would.

"Let me take that for you." He reached for the strap of her bag.

"Um." Leesa hesitated. She really didn't want her wallet to be too far from her in case she had to run for it. The clothes, the toothbrush, they were all things she could live without or replace, but not the cash. "Just let me grab something out of it first."

"Sure thing. I'll run out and get us two beers." He laughed. "And make sure that keg got inside somewhere out of sight."

"Thanks. A beer sounds really good." For the second time in a few minutes, Leesa was surprised by her own reaction. She wasn't a drinker, but after the day she'd had, and with all the feelings swirling through her, she could sure use a drink.

"Good." He flashed his pretty, white teeth at her. Then he was gone.

Leesa glanced around the room. It was obvious guys were occupying the space. Not much personal stuff was lying around, but what there was, was all over the floor. At least the beds were made, courtesy of housekeeping she was sure.

He'd be back in a second so she plopped her bag on the nearest bed and began digging through until she found her wallet buried deep in the bottom. She probably should have been carrying this on her the entire time anyway. This life, this world of hide and seek where the prize was her life, was all too new. She hoped she wasn't in it long enough to get used to it.

The door opened again and Chase entered, bearing two large red cups that matched the one Skeeter had been carrying. "Here you go."

She shoved the wallet in the front pocket of her oversized sweatshirt that bore the name of her college across the front in large black block letters. "Thanks."

Aside from the soda and pretzels she'd grabbed while waiting for Chase's signing thing to be over, she couldn't remember the last time she'd eaten. Probably last night before work. The cold, foamy beer slid down her throat easily. Too easily. Before Leesa knew it, the cup was mostly empty, and she'd only taken about three big gulps.

There was one chair, a desk and two beds. Realizing that, Leesa sat in the chair, then put her nearly empty cup down. Chase sat on the very end of the bed nearest her. The room wasn't huge so they were pretty close. Close enough she could see clearly the way his eyes kept zeroing in on her.

He sipped at his own cup. "Hey, you hungry? We can order up a pizza. We found a menu for a place that delivers."

She laughed, feeling lighter already. "Of course you did. What is it about men and pizza?"

"What?" He frowned. "It's the perfect food."

"And why is that?" This felt almost normal. Like the conversation any two attractive young people might have after just meeting. She flashed back to her and Chase's actual first meeting last night and remembered there was nothing typical or normal about it.

"It's got your carbs, vegetable and dairy—meat too if you

73

order it with toppings. You don't need a fork and knife, or even a plate to eat it. Napkins are optional, depending on how neat you want to be and if you're in mixed company. It comes in its own storage container, and—this is key—the leftovers are just as good cold the next morning when you wake up." He ticked off the last reason on his finger and grinned. "See? Perfect."

Leesa smiled. "You're right. It is perfect. I'd love some." She felt like she could really eat, and more than just pretzels. Being hungry was worlds better than the last twelve hours when all she felt like doing was throwing up.

"I'll find the number and call. Just give me a second." He glanced into her cup. "You need more beer."

"No. I don't think I should." She held up her hand.

He dismissed her protest with the wave of a hand and took her cup. "Don't be silly. It's a party. I'll call then get us refills."

She did notice he didn't make any move to bring her outside with him where the rest of the guys were, or even to bring them in. That was fine with her. She was far safer inside this room where it was quiet and they wouldn't attract the attention of security or any other hotel patrons who might complain about the noise. Or the keg. She shook her head.

A keg party in one of the nicer casino hotels in Vegas. An entire floor filled with cowboys with names like Chase, Garret and Skeeter. Just when she thought things couldn't get any stranger than her running for her life from her boss and his mobster brother, they did. Had she fallen down the rabbit hole?

The door opened again and halted her ponderings, but instead of Chase, Garret popped his head in. "Hey. Sorry. I just needed to grab something."

He moved to the mini fridge and pulled out a bottle of some sort of liquor and a few cans of soda. "I'm mixing up some bourbon and cola. Want one?"

"No. Thanks, though."

Garret glanced at her from his position near the fridge. "You know, you look kind of familiar. Were you at any of the competitions this weekend?"

Leesa wondered again what kind of competition he was talking about, but at least her other question was answered—he didn't remember her from last night. Did Chase?

She shook her head. "No. I wasn't."

He grinned, wide enough to rival Chase's usual expression. "Then you missed how great I rode."

"I'm afraid I did. Sorry."

Hands full, Garret shrugged. "That's okay. Come next door and I'll tell you all about it."

The door swung open again and Chase's return interrupted them. His eyebrows rose high beneath the brim of his cowboy hat when he saw Garret here talking to her. He pointedly stared at the items tenuously balanced in Garret's arms. "Got what you need?"

"Yup." Garret nodded but made no move to leave.

"Good. Let me get the door for you since your hands are full." With that, Chase effectively dismissed him.

Garret shot him a knowing look before treating Leesa to a grin. "See ya later. Come on over next door when you get bored here."

Chase looked like he wanted to kick Garret in the ass over that comment, but instead he said, "That girl you invited from the meet and greet just got off the elevator. I saw her going into Aaron and Skeeter's room."

"Really?" Garret's eyes opened wide.

"Yup." Chase nodded, a self-satisfied expression on his face.

Garret couldn't seem to get out of the room fast enough. The door slammed behind him and he hadn't even given them a backward glance.

Leesa laughed. "That must be some girl."

Chase handed her one of the two cups he'd had balanced in one hand. It was filled to the brim with foam. "Eh. She's his type. Not mine."

Leesa took a gulp of beer. Again it went down much too smoothly. She should really refill it with water from the bathroom sink and hydrate since she'd hardly drank anything for the past twenty-four hours. She hadn't realized how thirsty she was until she'd started drinking.

Feeling a bit lightheaded from lack of food and too much beer, she decided to ask the question uppermost on her mind, which was probably a bad idea. "What is your type?"

"You," he answered her with one word, but that was enough to send her heart reeling. Then he raised his cup to her in a silent toast and took a long gulp himself.

To think she'd assumed he was the shy, silent type. It was true he wasn't the biggest talker in the world, but when he did talk what he said could pack a real punch. She downed half the cup and wondered when the pizza would arrive. Then she realized that for the first time in over twelve hours, she'd actually forgotten about Jerry and Bruno and all the rest for a few minutes. Leesa wasn't sure if that was a good thing or a bad thing, and at the moment she didn't care.

"I ordered half-pepperoni and half-plain since I didn't know what you liked." Back on his perch at the end of the bed, Chase continued the conversation like Garret had never been there.

Leesa smiled. "You're too sweet."

"Don't let that fool you." His cherubic smile held a touch of the devil and she regretted not sitting on the bed next to him.

Maybe when the pizza came she'd remedy that.

Glancing over the rim of her big red cup at the cowboy opposite her, she took another sip. She had a feeling he wouldn't mind her joining him over there one bit.

"So..." The shy cowboy she'd first met last night was suddenly back in full force as he kicked the heel of his boot into the carpet. "The pizza should be here soon."

"Yup, I guess so. Thirty minutes or less. Right?" She actually smiled. How strange it felt. It was like the men chasing her were miles away when in reality they could be downstairs right now. Maybe it was the beer. Maybe it was being able to sit down and not have to keep moving, or being behind a closed door in private rather than in public. Or maybe it was Chase who made her feel this way. Whatever it was, she felt safe for the moment.

Jerry's order to get rid of her wouldn't go away, but for a little while she could pretend that the strip club and her life there didn't exist.

"Um, so about last night..." Chase's cheeks pinked in the shadow of his cowboy hat.

Maybe she wouldn't be able to pretend her life at the strip club didn't exist after all.

"Yeah?" Her heart fell. So much for her assuming, more like hoping, he hadn't recognized her. God, she was so stupid. Did he only invite her here for more sex?

"I was just wondering, hoping actually, that you came to the meet and greet today because you'd changed your mind."

Leesa's guard, which she'd led slip for a bit, flew right back up into place. "Changed my mind about what?"

"When I asked you out, you said you didn't date customers. I was kind of hoping you came to find me because you'd changed your mind about that. Or you know, if you haven't, maybe I could promise you I'd never be a customer again. Would that count?"

She couldn't help but laugh. Again he'd confused and surprised her. Could it be possible he was actually this nice and innocent? That he truly just wanted a date? "Why do you want to take me out, Chase?"

He drew in a long breath and let it out slowly. Then he stood and moved closer to her. Perching on the edge of the desk, he pushed both of their cups out of the way and then took her two hands in his. "I know what you're thinking."

"What am I thinking?" Her heart gave a little flutter. God, how she wanted him to really be this sweet. She hoped with all her might it wasn't all just a line to get her into bed.

"You're afraid that I only asked you out because of what happened between us at the end." His cheeks pinked but he maintained eye contact and remained totally serious.

"Did you?"

"No. I mean, don't get me wrong. You and me, together, it was pretty incredible..."

She smiled as he scrambled and blushed. He must have noticed her amused expression and smiled himself. "I know I look and sound like I just fell off the turnip truck."

Leesa laughed at that. "No... Okay. Yeah. Kind of."

"I know it might seem like I'm the type to fall for the first girl to show me any attention, but I have had some experience, you know, in that department."

She felt her brows rise at his declaration. "You're a cute guy, Chase. I'm sure lots of girls show you attention."

He rushed to continue. "I'm telling you that because I want you to know you and me...last night...that's not why I asked you out. I've been with women, doing lots more than what you and I did." His sudden stammer and red face was testament to the fact he didn't usually talk like this.

"Then why did you ask me out?" Her question sounded as filled with doubt as she felt.

Chase held her hands more tightly. "Because I like you"

"You don't know me." She shook her head.

"I know enough to see that I want to get to know more."

"It's not just because you want to finish what we started?"

He shook his head. "Oh, man. I'd be lying if I told you I haven't thought of that a hundred times since last night. I'd be crazy not to want to be with a woman as beautiful as you. But if all I wanted was to get laid, I could have picked up one of the girls at the meet and greet like some of the other guys did. No dinner necessary. Hell, no conversation either. It sounds bad, I know, but if that's what a guy is looking to do, bull riders hooking up with fans is pretty much a sure thing."

Of all the things he'd just confessed to her, and in spite of the relief she felt that he really wasn't being nice to her just to get into her pants, only one thing stood out in her mind. "Bull riders? You ride bulls?"

He laughed like she was joking, then stared at her closer, shock written clearly on his face. "You really didn't know?"

Leesa shook her head. "No. I assumed, I don't know, that you rode horses, I guess."

Chase grinned wide. "Good."

"Why good?"

"Because that means you weren't at the meet and greet to see any of the other bull riders because you're a fan. It means you really did come because you wanted to see me again. How did you know about it? Did one of the guys mention last night where we'd be today?"

"Yes, they did." Leesa wished it could be true. She felt bad lying, but she couldn't exactly confess she'd run into him accidentally while hiding for her life.

"I'm glad." He squeezed her hands. "You never answered me though. Have you changed your mind about our date?"

"I'm here, aren't I? We're going to be eating together soon." She glanced at her red cup nearby on the desk. "And we're having drinks. That sounds like a date to me, doesn't it?"

"Yeah, it does." He grinned until his eyes crinkled in the corners.

Damn, why did she suddenly have the urge to flirt with him? The same reason she wished they could go on a real date. She liked him. A lot.

"You even got me up to your room on our first date." She peered at him from beneath her lowered eyelashes. Meanwhile she wished this wouldn't have to be their one and only date.

Feeling moderately safe for the moment meant she was no longer able to ignore the extreme attraction between the two of them. Where the hell did she think this thing could go? Soon she'd have to find a way safely out of this town even though she still didn't know where she was going. She'd likely never see Chase again. That thought sucked.

"I did get you up here, didn't I?" Chase leaned in just a bit closer. "It must have been the tantalizing promise of beer and chips."

Leesa's gaze dropped to his lips and imagined how they would feel against hers. That was one thing they hadn't done last night. She'd felt him hard in her hand, felt him throb as he came, but she never felt his lips on hers. Suddenly, she really wanted to. The moment was right, or as right as it was going to get, as Chase leaned in even closer.

His mouth was soft against hers. His touch just hard enough to let her know he was willing to accept whatever she was willing to give, but that he definitely wanted more. She felt his shaky intake of breath as he tilted his head and worked his mouth against hers. She wished she tasted of toothpaste rather than beer, but he didn't seem to notice or mind as his hands moved from her hands and up her arms to finally settle on her face. He cupped her head like she was a porcelain doll he was afraid to break, but just as afraid to let go. She liked it.

He pulled away just enough to say, "I want you more than anything right now. That's why I'm going to stop kissing you."

"What?" That was the last thing she'd expected or wanted to hear from him.

"How else will you ever believe me that I asked you out because I like you and not because I'm looking to finish what we started?"

"Either you're as sincere as you seem, or you're the best liar with the best pickup lines I've ever met in my life."

Surprisingly, he grinned at that. "Sometimes I wish I was as quick at lines as some of the other guys, but I find it's easier to stick with the truth. Less likely to get bitten in the ass by one of your own lies that way."

Leesa smothered a sigh. If only she had the freedom of telling the truth right now without it getting herself or someone else killed. She smiled to lighten the mood again. "You're very smart for just a kid."

Chase's sandy brows rose. "A kid, huh?"

She grinned. "Yeah."

"I'll show you what a kid I am." His smile belied his tone as he leaned in again and did exactly what he promised. He kissed her with all the passion of a man. There was not one ounce of boy in him as he grabbed her head in his hands and claimed her mouth.

Then a knock sounded loudly on the door.

Leesa jumped and her heart began to race until she heard, "Pizza delivery."

Smiling, he stood. "Saved by the pizza."

"Yeah." Unfortunately.

Chapter Seven

For the second time in two days, Chase woke and had to pause a moment to take inventory. He hated waking up feeling like this. Wondering things like where was he? Why did his mouth taste like stale beer and pepperoni? What happened last night? More importantly, who was this warm body pressed up against him?

Holy crap! Eyes fully open and brain wide awake now, Chase glanced down at the woman by his side. It didn't take long for him to recognize the fall of long brown hair splayed across his chest. He breathed a sigh of relief.

Leesa. It all came rushing back to him.

He hadn't drunk that much last night. At least he didn't think so. He remembered he hadn't wanted to get too drunk in front of her. If things had gone anywhere with her, he wanted to be in top shape. More than that, he didn't trust the other guys around her if he passed out.

Chase had fallen asleep in his jeans and shirt, but he didn't think he'd passed out from alcohol, just from exhaustion since he hadn't been totally recovered from the night before. There was the memory of Garret and Skeeter, pretty inebriated themselves, busting through the door, demanding the last two pieces of pizza and then not leaving until Chase did a shot of bourbon with them. Or was it more like two or three shots?

Those two had talked Leesa's ear off about the competition and how great they'd both ridden, ninety percent of which were exaggerations. She'd listened politely and then even laughed when Skeeter sang the song that had gotten him his nickname.

Leesa had drank the two beers he'd brought her. Then Garret had handed her another cup when he came in for the pizza. That might have had bourbon and coke though, instead of beer in it.

Damn. Chase should have paid closer attention to what he'd given her. Garret could have made it super strong for all Chase knew. He glanced at the sleeping figure next to him. No wonder she still slept so soundly. Poor thing.

After Garret and Skeeter's intrusion, once he'd finally convinced them to leave, they'd turned on the television for a bit. Leesa had looked tired and had drunk too much for him to let her leave, not that she was trying to go anywhere. She seemed perfectly content to sit in the room with him. Then what? He supposed they'd fallen asleep right there on the bed. The television was off now. Had he turned it off last night? Had she? He didn't remember.

He really had to quit drinking, because he was pretty tired of piecing together the night before the next morning. All he was sure of now was that there hadn't been any more than those two kisses right before the pizza came. If there had been more, he would remember it without a doubt.

Leesa still breathed with the steady, deep rhythm of sleep. Not wanting to disturb her, he slipped his body out from beneath her. She let out a little moan and rolled over, snuggling into the pillow. He regretted getting out of bed more than he could have imagined, but nature called. Maybe he could slip back into bed when he was done without waking her. That was a really nice idea.

He touched his head. Not so bad. No headache. No hangover. Yeah, he was tired and a little groggy, but that could be the early hour. Judging by the grey light filtering through the curtains, the sun had barely risen. Then again, this was Las Vegas. That glow coming through the window could be caused by neon, not nature.

Chase shook his head as he stumbled toward the bathroom. He'd be happy to get back to his family's farm. This life was exciting. Travel. A different city every week. But he'd be happy to have his mama's home cooking every day, and be able to cleanse his system of all the junk food and alcohol he'd indulged in lately. He'd work out daily at home and come back next season leaner and meaner and ready to win.

That resolution made, Chase took care of what he had to in the bathroom, including a quick shower. He decided it was best to be clean in case Leesa woke up feeling amorous. You never know, and it didn't hurt to be prepared.

After brushing his teeth, Chase eased open the bathroom door.

She was still asleep. Good. He could creep back into bed and she'd never know he was gone. Even if they hadn't had sex, he still liked waking up next to her. It felt nice.

With one of the hotel's white towels wrapped around his waist, Chase tiptoed into the room. They'd fallen asleep last night with the lights on, so he'd have no problem finding a pair of shorts in the clean clothes piled in his duffle bag. He would put those on instead of getting back into his jeans. Might as well be comfortable, and as far as access in case Leesa was a morning person, shorts were far better than jeans. Hell, a man could dream, couldn't he?

Chase found a pair of boxer shorts, but decided that was too intimate. He had a feeling she might not like waking up to find him in underwear in bed with her. It would make him seem damn presumptuous. In spite of the fact they'd done stuff together at the club, he wasn't about to assume anything because of it.

She was different here, off work. Besides, the strip club and that lap dance had been part of her job. Chase didn't want to be a job. He wanted her to like him, to want him, to be with him because she wanted to, not because someone paid her to.

He dug farther into the jumbled heap, looking for a pair of his workout shorts to wear. Unfortunately, with home just a day away, most of his clothes were dirty. He'd gotten lazy and figured he could bring his laundry there and wash it more easily than locate a laundromat.

This was Vegas. There were far better ways to spend his time than to sit and watch his clothes spin in circles. One such way was snoring lightly in his bed. That thought made him smile, and he dug with more enthusiasm than before. Hell, if he had to, he'd grab a pair of Garret's shorts. The guy had more clothes than most girls.

Chase turned toward Garret's side of the room intent on pilfering some shorts when something shiny caught his eye. On the dresser, right in front of the mirror and below the lamp sat two gold rings.

"What the hell?" Chase moved closer and picked one up, then the second. One was tiny, the other large enough to fit on his finger. Then he spied the pieces of paper lying beneath the rings. He picked up the smaller one. It was a receipt for one wedding ceremony and two gold bands, paid for in cash with yesterday's date.

Swallowing hard, Chase picked up the larger, more decorative piece of paper. Across the top, in fancy printing was written *Certificate of Marriage*. Below that, under the word groom was—holy crap—his name printed in block letters. His eyes swung to the bride's name and there it was—Leesa Santiago. No, he'd never heard her last name, but the Leesa had two E's in it and how often did you see that?

He scanned down the page and saw again yesterday's date and a line with his signature. Next to that was what must be Leesa's signature, and beneath that were two scrawled names he didn't recognize listed under Witnesses. Chase ran his hand over his face, rubbing hard.

He hadn't drank that much. How the hell could he have been intoxicated enough to get married? And how could he not remember doing it? He was still standing in the towel, probably with his mouth hanging open, when Leesa began to stir in the bed. He turned and saw her sit up slowly.

Sleepily, she stretched. "Morning. Sorry about last night. We both fell asleep watching TV."

The rings and certificate still in his hand, Chase swallowed hard. "Apparently that's not all we did."

She frowned. "What do you mean?"

"You don't remember either?" Her clothes from the night before were still completely on, just as his had been. So even if they had somehow stumbled downstairs drunk, then out into the street to find a twenty-four hour wedding chapel, they likely hadn't come home to have sex after. He was happy about that. Not remembering getting hitched was one thing, but he really would like to remember the first time they had sex.

As she stared at him with confusion, the full ramifications of what they'd done began to hit him. They were married. Legally bound in the eyes of the law and the state of Nevada. Man and wife.

What would Leesa think about it when he finally told her what they'd done? Would she freak out? And why wasn't he freaking out more himself?

That was something to think about.

Married. Wow.

Hell, as long as they had already done it, he wouldn't mind trying it out for a little bit. Like on a trial basis, just to get the feel of it. Hmm, and they could legally and morally have all the sex they wanted. That part was pretty good.

She rose from the bed and padded across the room in just her socks. He did remember suggesting she take her shoes off so she could get comfortable when they were sitting on the bed watching television. Come to think of it, he'd woken up without his boots. Glancing at the door, he saw them sitting there right where he remembered leaving them last night.

Did they take their vows last night drunk and barefoot?

Maybe if the two of them combined their memories they could put the pieces of this mystery together. Should they ask the other guys if they knew what had happened? Somehow the dead last thing Chase wanted to do was admit any of this to Garret.

Had Garret plied them both with shots last night until they were so drunk they did this? If that were the case, Chase would really have to kill him this time. That was for later. Right now, Chase had to break the bad news—or possibly good news, depending on how you looked at it—to his bride.

A picture was worth a thousand words, or in this case, a marriage license was. He thrust the certificate at her. She took it and frowned as she looked it over, then her eyes opened wide. Her gaze shot to him. "Where did you get this?"

"It was lying right here when I woke up. Along with that receipt and these." He held up the rings. He slipped the larger one onto the fourth finger of his left hand. "It fits." Not perfectly, it was a little tight, but it was on his finger and once his body wasn't soaked in beer, it would probably fit pretty well.

He held the smaller one up for her to see. He watched as her throat worked. Slowly, he reached out, took her left hand and slid the ring onto her finger. It was a tad bit big on her and spun a little too easily, but it stayed on her finger without falling off when she held her hand down to stare at it. Her hands were so small, it was probably the smallest size they had on short notice.

"Yours fits too."

With them both wearing their wedding bands, this was starting to feel really real now.

She glanced down at the ring, then the paper in her hand.

"How?" She looked up at him and shook her head.

Chase shook his own head. "I don't know. I didn't think we drank that much."

Her eyes flew open. "Oh my God!"

"What?" It felt like his heart flew into his throat.

"Last night. After we both fell asleep watching television, I woke up. I had a horrible headache but all I had with me were those over the counter painkillers that have sleeping stuff in them. I got up and took two of those pills."

"So?" Chase frowned. "That wouldn't make you sleepwalk into a wedding chapel and drag me with you. Would it?"

He shouldn't have used the word drag. If he had gone along with her, he had a feeling he went willingly.

"I don't know. It might have." There was panic in her voice. "Haven't you seen those commercials for prescription sleep aids? Where they warn you that taking the product can cause driving or eating at night with no memory of the event?"

Having spent too much time in hotel rooms watching television, yeah, he had seen those commercials. He just never thought it actually happened. "Okay, maybe that would explain you not remembering, but it doesn't explain my—"

His lack of recollection would have to wait because she had gone pale. Leesa reached out for the corner of the dresser. He grabbed both of her arms to support her. He'd never seen a woman actually faint before, but he had a feeling this was what they looked like right before they did.

She wasn't handling this as well as he'd hoped. If he was perfectly honest, he'd admit he wasn't sorry it had happened. He wanted to get to know Leesa better. Much better. From their one-sided talk last night, where he'd asked her personal questions and she'd mostly avoided answering them, he realized if he didn't find a way to keep her around a little longer he'd probably never see her again.

This was one hell of a messed up way to do that, but he'd take what opportunity he could get. If he could just convince her to stay with him until they could investigate getting a divorce or annulment or whatever people who woke up married in Vegas got, he could maybe win her trust once she got to know him.

He hadn't planned on a wife, and after they straightened things out, he wouldn't have one. A girlfriend was an entirely different story though. Having a girlfriend on the road was a challenge. Chase knew that. But other riders made it work. Mustang. Slade. They both had serious steady girlfriends. Chase wanted that. He was pretty sure he wanted to give it a try with Leesa.

Meanwhile, right now he had to calm the panic he saw rising in her. "Listen. I have an idea."

Seeming so much smaller and more helpless than she had when she was strutting in her high heels around on stage, she looked up at him. "What?"

This was the real Leesa he was seeing now. Insecure. Scared. Though he suspected the bold side of her, the one she showed on stage, was inside her somewhere too. The thought of unleashing it, of witnessing the two parts together, had him tingling inside. She was half-devil, half-angel, and he was man enough to handle them both. If she'd only give him a chance to prove that. Which brought him to his plan...

"I was going to leave for home today. I have my truck. I'm not driving with anyone else this time so I'll be alone. You come with me. My uncle is a lawyer. He lives in the same town as my parents. We'll bring these papers and explain to him what happened. He'll know what to do about it. Okay?"

Still looking dazed, she nodded. "Okay."

Chase suppressed a whoop of joy. He didn't know what had happened last night, or how they'd ended up standing here with gold bands and a license between them, but he intended on taking advantage of the gift he'd been given. Time. That's all he needed.

Sure, they'd straighten out the mess and undo the marriage, but a lot could happen between Vegas and Oklahoma. Chase couldn't wait to find out what.

Chapter Eight

The hot water sluiced off Leesa's back, and with it, a few days worth of fear and worry. She wasn't out of the woods by any means, but going with Chase to Oklahoma, even if it was as his bride, gave her some breathing room. If she kept her head down, she'd be safe for a while staying with his family until they figured out how to reverse this marriage.

How the hell had they ended up married anyway? She supposed she could write it off to not enough food, too much alcohol for both of them, and one sleep aid on her part. She probably shouldn't have taken that at all. What if Bruno had come busting through the door and she was drugged and groggy? Though she'd taken them before and been able to wake up just fine when needed, and never to her knowledge had she sleepwalked to a chapel and gotten married. At least not until last night.

Oh well. Of all the men in the world she could have gotten accidentally married to, Chase would be her first choice. At least she didn't end up accidentally married to someone like Jerry. Even the thought of him made her stomach churn.

Things could be far worse. She knew that too well. Married and alive was much better than single and dead.

Leesa poured another handful of hotel shampoo into her palm and lathered her hair. The tiny bottle was almost empty now, but Chase had already showered and Garret would have to be on his own. Besides, these guys rode bulls. Real cowboys could use hand soap on their hair in a pinch, she supposed. Leesa shook her head at her own thoughts. Just the fact she was worrying about shampoo rather than dying proved how different this morning was compared to yesterday.

A bit of conditioner, another rinse and Leesa's hair was clean. Flipping the faucet, she turned off the water, stepped out of the shower stall and onto the bath mat. She grabbed a towel from the rack and spied Chase's razor lying on the sink. She hadn't thought much about him shaving. Of course he did. He was an adult male. She could attest to that first hand.

The image tantalized her. Chase wiping the steam from the mirror. Lathering his cheeks and chin. Standing in nothing but a towel.

He'd looked pretty damn good in that towel this morning. It had been the first thing she'd noticed before he'd distracted her with the marriage certificate and two gold bands, one of which was still wrapped around the fourth finger on her left hand. She glanced at it again.

Wow. Married. Even if it was only temporary, they were still married.

She eyed Chase's razor again and then on a spur of the moment whim, braced one ankle on the sink. She ran it quickly over her shin and knee. It wasn't the best shaving job, but eventually she had both legs and both underarms mostly stubble free.

Guiltily she rinsed the blades off well. Guys hated when women used their razors to shave their legs. At least her ex had. Leesa pushed that unpleasant memory away. That was long over and if she never thought of him again, it would be too soon.

She dried and then put the razor back where she'd found it. The entire time she tried not to think that she'd shaved just in case something happened with Chase. It was going to be a long drive to his home in Oklahoma. Both of them in the cab of his truck for hours and hours... She should be worrying about other things besides the possibility they might have sex. Then again, why shouldn't they? They were married.

Temporarily, she reminded herself one more time as she hung her head upside down and rubbed the water out of her hair with the towel.

She'd brought a change of clothes into the bathroom with her so she could dress in private. As Leesa pulled on her bra and underwear, the irony wasn't lost on her. She'd stripped nearly naked in front of both Chase and his friends on stage, but here she didn't even want him to see her in just the towel. Keeping her life compartmentalized had been the only thing to keep her sane these past few months. It had been what had allowed her to distance herself enough to do what she'd done with Chase in the back room. Then again, she hadn't remained very distant, had she?

A fluttering started low in her belly when she remembered what she'd felt between her and Chase in that back room, and then again last night when he'd kissed her. Yeah, sure. Compartmentalized. *Ha!* She'd been a woman attracted to a man. Chase had not been just another customer. Now she was married to him. She smothered the guilt. Maybe her subconscious had sleepwalked her medicated body and his drunk one all the way to the chapel on purpose.

Leesa sighed. They'd straighten it all out. Until then she'd get to see Oklahoma and get out of Vegas with her life intact. Chase didn't seem to be complaining about the surprise nuptials. They'd just both have to make the best of it.

With that thought firmly in place, she pulled on the last of her clothing and opened the bathroom door. A burst of steam preceded her into the bedroom where she found Chase balling up his clothes and shoving them into his bag. Resisting the urge to go over and fold them neatly for him, Leesa went to her own bag and put her neatly stacked pile of yesterday's clothes into it.

"I figure we'll pack, grab something to eat, then come up, get our bags and hit the road."

Leesa stopped zipping her bag midway. "Um, do you think we could get on the road first, and then stop at a truck stop or something and get breakfast to go? Maybe egg sandwiches? Something easy to eat in the truck."

He looked at her with surprise then smiled. "You are determined not to let me buy you a decent meal in a real restaurant, aren't you?"

"No. That's not it—"

"I have money you know, if that's what you're worried about. I know I haven't been riding my best this year, but I've still done good. I can afford to buy you a nice meal. I promise."

Again, she wasn't sure exactly how he earned money riding bulls, or how much one could earn doing that, but she supposed during the long trip together she had plenty of time to find out. "I believe you, Chase. You can buy me a meal when we get where we're going. For right now, I'm kind of anxious to get on the road."

He seemed to look too deeply into her, the way he had a habit of doing. Though maybe it was her own guilt about hiding things from him and using him to escape that made her feel that way. Finally, he nodded. "Okay. We can get on the road first and stop later. No problem."

She nodded, happy he'd agreed so easily but still feeling like she needed an explanation to cover herself. "Thanks. It's just I think I've had enough of this town for a while. You know? I'm anxious to get away. Start my vacation."

Again, he watched her. "Understood. I'm warning you though, Oklahoma isn't exactly the vacation capital of the world. My hometown's got a few thousand people in it and that's it. The highlight of the town was when the diner decided to stay open until eleven at night on weekends. We've got a movie theater that shows one movie at a time, not ten like the ones they have in the cities. And if you want to go shopping at a real mall, you have to take a road trip and make a day out of it."

Leesa laughed. "It sounds perfect to me." Funny thing was she meant every word.

He looked at her strangely again, laughing himself. "All right. If you say so." Chase glanced around the room. "Is that everything?"

Smothering her guilt, she thought she felt her cheeks heat. Leesa shook her head. "Your razor is still on the sink in the bathroom."

"That's Garret's, but thanks anyway."

"Oh." Now she felt really bad for using it. Chase grabbed both his bag and hers and moved toward the door. As she glanced back at the room, still strewn with Garret's stuff, it killed Leesa not to do her usual hotel room check, pulling out every drawer in both the dresser and night stand, kneeling down to look under the bed for socks or shoes that may have gotten kicked underneath. "Um, don't you want to check one more time in case you left anything?"

And she'd told Chase she was the kind of girl to go with the flow. Yeah right.

Chase shook his head. "Nah. If I missed anything, Garret will grab it for me. Which reminds me. I should really wake them up next door and tell them I'm leaving."

He glanced down at his left hand. "Huh. Maybe not. I think maybe I shouldn't let them know about what happened."

"I think you're right. You have the um...paperwork. Right? Your uncle may need it."

"Got it folded up safe in my wallet." Chase patted the front pocket of his jeans.

"Good."

He glanced at the clock next to the bed and cringed. "It's early still, and those guys were pretty plastered last night. Maybe I'll just leave Garret a note. Or text him later from the road."

Watching him make excuses, she smiled. "You don't want to lie to him."

Chase laughed. "Hell no. I've lied to him before, about you for instance. I just don't feel like dealing with them right now."

"Okay. Your choice." Leesa didn't quite believe him.

Chase put both bags down and bent over the desk. He scribbled something on the pad of paper lying next to the phone. Leesa did her best not to stare at his butt in his jeans as he did. When he straightened again, she wrestled her gaze back to his face.

"Okay. Done. Ready?" He waited for her answer.

She nodded. "Ready.'

"Then let's go."

With a surge of adrenaline, Leesa followed Chase out into the hall, holding her breath the entire walk to the elevator. When the door slid open and she saw past Chase that it was occupied but she couldn't see by whom, her breath caught in her throat. She didn't breath freely again until Chase dropped the bags on the floor and shook the hand of the cowboy who stepped out.

"Mustang."

"Hey, Chase. You heading out?"

"Yup, we are." Chase nodded. He moved to the side and took a small step back so he was standing next to her. "This is Leesa."

The man named Mustang—bull riders sure had strange names—tipped his cowboy hat to her. "Nice to meet you."

"You too." She nodded and managed to answer past the lump that had lodged in her throat when she had thought maybe Bruno and the goons were on the elevator. She had a feeling that fear would stay with her all the way to Oklahoma, if not forever.

Meanwhile, the cowboy's eyes had dropped to her left hand and she saw his eyebrows rise at the sight of the wedding band that, ridiculously, she was still wearing. They should probably take them off. It wasn't like the marriage was real or anything. She supposed she was afraid she'd lose the band if she did take it off and stuck it in her pocket.

The cowboy's eyes moved to Chase, who had noticed where his friend was looking too. "Um. We'll talk later."

Mustang nodded. "I think we probably should." Then his eyes caught the glint on Chase's hand and they flew open wider. "Yeah. We definitely need to talk."

Chase laughed. "I know. I'll call you."

"You do that." The cowboy tipped his hat to her. "Ma'am." Then he was gone.

Chase pushed the button to open the elevator doors again, since they'd long since closed during the strange exchange between the two men.

She waited once more with bated breath for the elevator to arrive, hoping with all her might that it was empty and that the search for her had moved elsewhere. She glanced up at Chase's profile. "You know, we can take these rings off so you don't have to keep explaining them."

"I know." He looked down at her but made no move to take his off.

"You don't want to?"

"Nope." Chase shook his head decisively.

"Why not?"

"Because I kind of like how it feels on." With a grin, he scooped the bags off the floor as the doors slid open again. Then waited for her to get in first.

"Oh, okay." She considered that as she stepped inside.

Chase stepped in after her and then pushed the button for one of the parking levels. Good. They weren't going through the casino. "That all right with you?"

"Uh. Yeah."

He leaned down and planted a gentle kiss on her lips and her stomach gave another flutter.

"Good."

Huh. This gave her entirely something else to consider.

"How long will it take us to get to your place?"

"It's about a sixteen-hour drive, not counting any stops we make. I figure we'll drive maybe ten hours today, find a hotel for the night, then knock out the rest tomorrow. We'll be home in time for dinner with my family. My mama's the best cook. I'll call her and tell her you're coming and to make something special." He smiled at her.

Cat Johnson

A hotel for the night. A special dinner with his family. Leesa swallowed hard. "Okay."

It was going to be interesting.

Chapter Nine

He had sixteen hours alone with her in the truck to convince her they should give getting to know each other better a try. Actually, that wasn't exactly true. They also had tonight in the hotel room.

All alone, all night long. Sure they had been together in his room last night, but there was always the threat of Garret busting through the door with Skeeter and Aaron, not to mention Aaron's brother in tow to disturb them.

All night alone in a hotel room with Leesa, and they were married. Legally married. Legally allowed to have sex. All night long. He remembered he had promised her he'd have his uncle take care of the divorce as soon as possible. He shot a sideways glance at her across the cab of the truck. Maybe he could convince his uncle to drag his feet for a little bit. Just long enough for Leesa to realize they should at least give dating each other a chance.

Chase was tired of being single. He wouldn't mind trying the girlfriend thing out for a little while. Perhaps for a nice long while. He had a feeling he'd like it. Hell, being temporarily married wasn't so bad at all. Being in a relationship—an adult one, not the kind he'd had in high school—had to be the same.

Except for now they were married and not just dating. He shot her a look again. Visions of waking up next to Leesa every morning filled his head instead of the view of the road in front of him. Her hair would be all messy, splayed across his chest and the pillow like it had been this morning.

Yeah, he could get used to that.

Just as he was fantasizing his cell phone rang. Glancing at the caller ID, Chase saw Garret's name appear. He groaned softly.

"Who is it?"

"Garret."

"Aren't you going to answer it?"

"And tell him what?"

"I don't know. That you wanted to hit the road early to get home and didn't have time to hang around until he woke up."

"I wrote that in the note. Besides, he's going to want to talk about...stuff."

"What kind of stuff?"

Chase pressed his lips together considering his options here and decided honesty was the best policy. "About you."

"Me?"

"Yeah. Look, I know it's wrong but guys talk about stuff. You know. Girls. He's going to want to know if anything happened. Between you and me, I mean." Chase hated telling her that. It made it sound like guys always discussed their conquests the next day. Unfortunately, in Garret's case it was true. He could tell by the silence radiating loudly off her that she was unhappy with that revelation. "I didn't tell him anything about the other night."

"You didn't?" Her voice held a good amount of doubt.

"No."

"Why not?"

"Because it's none of his business for one. And because I...I don't know. I didn't want to." It would have cheapened what had been a pretty nice moment. On top of that, Chase really did want to see her again, and if they had started dating, he didn't need Garret and the rest of the guys knowing what had happened between them the night they'd met.

Chase nearly laughed. He definitely hadn't figured they'd end up married. Now he really didn't want the guys knowing what had gone on with him and his bride. And he didn't need any shit from them about waking up married in Vegas. Nope, it was best to let ringing phones lie.

Meanwhile, Leesa was watching him with a strange expression. He frowned. "What?"

"Thank you for not telling them." Her voice sounded soft and full of sincerity.

He tried to dismiss her gratitude with a casual shrug. "I'm not the type to kiss and tell, but you're welcome."

Chase glanced across the truck and was treated to a small smile from her, before she turned to stare out the side window at the passing scenery. His heart, and parts lower, tightened. Damn, he really, really hoped she didn't ask him to book two rooms tonight. Sure, he would do it if she asked, but he truly hoped she didn't.

"You know, I didn't think you recognized me yesterday afternoon." Leesa's comment broke into a very nice fantasy about what married life would be like.

What she'd said finally registered with the part of his brain not occupied with thinking about sex. "Why wouldn't I have recognized you?"

"You didn't say that you did when I came up to your table." She laughed. "And I wasn't exactly dressed the same as the other night."

He let out a laugh of his own. "No, you weren't, but I knew who you were. Even with the hat, I'd recognize your face anywhere. Then when you talked to me, I knew for sure. I remembered your voice..."

Chase's cock stirred at the memory of her outfit at the strip club. The way she had danced only for him on stage. Her voice in his ear when she'd told him to relax and enjoy it, then called him cowboy. He swallowed hard. If he didn't stop this, his dick would be able to take the wheel and steer for him.

He glanced from the road to her face, which was turned toward him. Her cheeks pinked and her eyelids dropped for a second before she brought her gaze back up to meet his. Chances were she was remembering the same things he was. His hands guiding her hips. The way she shook in his arms when she came.

They sped by a sign along the side of the highway for a fast-food restaurant. Chase cleared his throat and wrestled his mind away from the fantasy of what it would be like to take her breast in his mouth and tease the nipple until it peaked. "Hungry?"

She nodded. "Yeah, I am. Can we go through the drive-through window instead of going inside?"

"Sure. You don't need to stop for, uh, you know, anything?" How ridiculous was that? They'd been nearly naked together, he'd come in her hand, but he found himself getting embarrassed asking if she needed to use the bathroom.

Leesa shook her head. "No. Thanks." She dropped her gaze again. They were both feeling that they were strangers. Married strangers. It was a very strange sensation.

He already knew the sex stuff was great between them. Hopefully by the end of this trip they'd be more comfortable with each other as far as the everyday normal stuff. Like boyfriends and girlfriends were with each other. Or husbands and wives.

Chase flipped on his blinker and slowed for the exit ramp. Tractor trailers lined the shoulder. He drove past them and followed the signs for the drive-through lane.

He stopped by the menu sign. "What's your pleasure?" He knew what he'd like to be eating at the moment and it wasn't on that big lit-up menu, but he tried not to think of that.

"Just a breakfast sandwich and a cup of coffee. Thanks." She began digging in her bag. She finally emerged with a five-dollar bill and thrust it at him.

Chase frowned. "Don't worry about it. I got it."

"No, really. I want to pay my own way."

This was not good. When a woman wouldn't even let a man buy her a damn fast-food breakfast sandwich it meant she wasn't interested. That she didn't want to owe him anything.

He felt his hopes hit the ground as he shook his head and pushed her hand away.

"Really. It's fine. You won't owe me anything. I swear." That had come out sounding a bit harsh. He pursed his lips and mustered up an apology. "Sorry."

He moved the truck up to the window and ordered, then pulled to the second window to pay and wait for their order, avoiding eye contact with her the entire time.

After he handed her the bag full of food so he could roll up the window and pull away, she finally spoke. "I already owe you more than you know."

He frowned. Pulling the truck into an open spot, he threw it into park and turned in his seat. Was she finally ready to explain all the strangeness he'd noticed with her? The nerves. The aversion to any place public. Always keeping one eye on the nearest exit like she might need to escape. "Why?"

She shrugged and shook her head at the same time, suddenly very busy arranging the food inside the bag in her lap.

"Here." Leesa thrust a hash brown at him. He took it from her and laid it on the dashboard. Another hash brown and his own breakfast sandwich came his way. She put her coffee in the cup holder. "Thank you for breakfast."

"You're welcome." He stifled a huff. She wasn't talking. He could wait her out. He was a patient man, but he wasn't going to put up with her paying her own way. He was a gentleman after all. If Leesa's secret had anything to do with finances, she may need to hold on to any money she had. "Am I going to have to convince you to let me buy you lunch and dinner too?"

"Probably." She kept her eyes down, focused on unwrapping her food.

Chase reached along the back of the seat and let his fingertips brush her shoulder. "Why?"

Leesa finally looked up at him, a small apologetic smile on her lips. "Because I'm stubborn."

He cocked a brow in doubt. "That's the only reason?"

She drew in a deep breath. "Chase, I've been on my own for a while now. I'm not used to anyone doing things for me."

"Well, while you're with me, you better get used to it." Feeling moderately better, he waited for her response. This wasn't like a girl who ordered chicken instead of lobster because she had no intention of putting out for her date after he paid for dinner. This was definitely something else. Leesa was into him, he was certain. It was whatever else was up with her that was getting in between them.

She finally nodded and mumbled, "Okay. I'll try."

"Good." He turned back around in his seat and got busy

devouring the meal.

Hopefully she'd allow them to actually sit down and get some decent food at one point during the trip. In any case, his mama's food was going to be very welcome by the time they got home.

The miles and the hours passed, and so did other more personal milestones, such as the first time she touched his arm and asked quietly if they could stop at a rest area. One barrier crossed. Many more to go.

Sometimes they sat in silence and listened to the songs on the radio, until they drove out of range and static took over. Then he'd ask her to find them another station.

Other times they talked, but never about anything really serious. Like when she asked him to explain bull riding to her.

At first he wasn't sure what she meant. What was to explain? You got on the bull. You tried not to get bucked off. Then once he got into it, he realized there was much more to explain, especially for someone who hadn't been around it their entire life the way he had.

He explained the bull score and the rider score. What it meant to challenge the four judges' decision and how much it cost a rider if their challenge was overturned. He told her the reasons a rider could get awarded a reride and also how he could be disqualified.

Before he knew it, it was long past time for lunch and closer to dinner. It was the fading light of day that first signaled him to that fact, followed closely by the grumbling of his stomach.

"Thank you." He glanced at Leesa across the dim interior of the truck.

She frowned. "For what?"

"For keeping me company. This ride is pretty agonizing when I do it alone. You made the time fly by." Chase was finding it hard to keep his mind on the road the nearer they got to stopping for the night.

"Good. I'm glad." Leesa smiled at him. He loved when she smiled.

He grinned back and decided to use the situation to his advantage. Maybe he could get her to agree to let him get them some decent food for tonight. "So, as you can see, I owe you and I'm going to take you out to a nice dinner."

She frowned again and started to shake her head.

Determined, Chase shook his right back at her. "Nope. I won't take no for an answer this time."

"I don't have anything to wear for a nice dinner."

He didn't believe that excuse for a second. "I'm in jeans and cowboy boots."

"Every male around here is in jeans and cowboy boots. It's different for females. I'm in a sweatshirt and sneakers. Maybe we could get some really nice takeout and eat it in our hotel room instead?"

Chase wasn't about to argue with that, especially since she'd said *our* hotel room instead of your room, or my room. Our room. He smiled. "Okay. Sounds good."

Leesa looked happier. Chase definitely was happy. He began keeping is eye peeled for a town that would offer both a decent hotel and a restaurant with takeout.

Cheap hotels he was good at finding. He and the guys had stayed at enough of those. Really nice hotels could be few and far between on the open road, even when he'd had a good enough year to afford staying in one. Luckily, last year had been a very good year and this year hadn't gone so badly either. He had been in a bit of a sophomore slump in the beginning, but he'd finished strong. He'd made decent money. More than enough to treat Leesa well for the two days he had her with him. Hopefully good enough to convince her to stick around for longer.

Finally Chase saw a sign that looked promising. Heart in his throat just thinking about how close he was to getting Leesa out of this truck and into a hotel room, he flipped on his blinker and pulled from the left lane into the right.

The two miles between the exit sign and the actual turn off seemed to crawl by, but eventually the exit was before him. He followed the hotel-and-food sign at the end of the ramp and turned right onto a route that may have a number as a name, but looked more like a country road. That was fine, as long as it led him to where he wanted to go. That being a place to get decent food for their belly and a nice bed for...other things.

Chase reminded himself that Leesa may not want other things. After a day in the tight confines of the truck with her that would be tough. Just listening to her voice got him hard half the time. Must be one of those Pavlovian things he'd learned about in school. His body associated her voice with extreme pleasure and reacted every time he heard it. Fine with him, though he'd like to experience that pleasure again and not just the constant hard-on.

He wrestled his mind off his bawdy thoughts and started to look for the hotel and food the sign had promised. Eventually he saw what looked like a country inn. He slowed and pulled into the parking lot, eyeing the building suspiciously. These kinds of places were hit or miss. They could be clean and cheap with a charm you didn't find in the large chain hotels, or they could be run-for-your-life horrible.

It was the kind of place where you parked your vehicle right in front of whatever room you got. There were soda machines under an awning that sheltered the walkway along the building. The more he looked at it, the more he feared this wasn't the best place for them to stay. If it were him alone, or him, Garret and Skeeter, that would be a totally different story. Hell, they'd slept in the truck in a pinch. But this night had potential to be pretty special and he didn't want something like cockroaches or a dirty bathroom to ruin it. Even just thinking that put a damper on what had been a pretty happy erection.

He turned in his seat toward Leesa. "What do you think? Should we give it a try?"

She glanced around the parking lot. "There are no other cars here."

"I know. That worries me a little."

"It's fine. Can you go in and get the room? Maybe one in the back. So it's quiet and we won't hear the traffic all night long?"

Chase glanced in the rearview mirror at the road in question. There was no traffic. In fact, he'd seen barely a handful of cars on it since getting off the highway. He didn't question her though, only nodded. "Okay. Whatever you want. You sure you don't want me to ask if we can see one of the rooms first before we check in?"

"Nope. I'm not picky."

He laughed. Then she was the only girl in the world who wasn't. He didn't say that but nodded. "Sure you don't want to come inside with me?"

"I'm good. I'll just wait here." Her gaze shot to the side mirror before she turned back to him and smiled, an expression that looked forced.

Chase stifled a sigh. In between all his sexual fantasies, he'd forgotten there was something else going on with her. He'd have to devote some time to getting to the bottom of that. At least as much time as he devoted to getting to the bottom of her...so to speak.

"All right. I'll be right back." He turned off the ignition, swung his door open and slid out of the driver's seat. Feeling stiff from sitting for so long, he stretched. The gold of his wedding band caught the light. He wondered how long it took a person to get used to seeing a ring on his finger. Probably longer than he'd be married to Leesa.

With that deadline hanging over his head, Chase walked with renewed energy toward the office and rang the bell on the desk with probably more enthusiasm than necessary.

Chapter Ten

Leesa stabbed her plastic fork into the remaining rice that had come with their Tex-Mex takeout order. "This is really good."

Chase glanced up from his own Styrofoam box, his white fork looking tiny in his hand. "Yeah."

She noted his scowl. "You don't like it?"

"I like it fine, but one day I'd like to eat a meal with you off a real plate with an actual fork."

"I thought the lack of plates and forks was half the reason you love pizza."

"Pizza is different."

If she wasn't mistaken he was pouting a little. She smiled. "Really, Chase. I'm fine here."

"I know you are. What I don't know is why you won't let me take you out to a real place."

Besides trying to keep them both alive, she didn't have a good reason so she skirted the question. "You'll have real plates and forks to eat off tomorrow when we get to your parents' house."

"I guess." He sneered a bit at that but still managed to look adorable. By the time he got to his last rib from his dinner, it was obvious he'd had enough with the plastic ware. He abandoned the fork and picked up the bone in his hands, tearing a hunk of meat off with his teeth. After he'd swallowed the mouthful, he glanced down at her takeout container and grinned. "I'm glad you liked your fajitas."

Looking down, she laughed. All that remained of her meal was some parsley garnish. "It was good and I was really hungry."

"You should have asked me to stop earlier." This man was determined to feed her.

"I didn't notice I was hungry until I saw the food."

"Yeah, I get like that too."

They had more in common than she would have ever guessed a bull-riding cowboy from Oklahoma and a college dropout turned stripper from the West Coast would ever have. During their road trip she'd discovered they shared the same taste in music—classic rock with some modern country thrown in. They had the same taste in food. Even during the day-long drive, she was just as comfortable riding in silence with him as when they were having a conversation. In fact, considering the situation she'd been fairly relaxed all day, until they'd walked into the room. Then she realized just how small a room seemed when it was filled with Chase and two beds.

Though the fact he'd asked for a room with two beds spoke to exactly how much of a gentleman he really was, which made her want to crawl right into one of those beds with him, that would probably be a bad idea. They were on their way to get a divorce, after which she'd have to figure out where to go and what to do with her life that wouldn't get her killed.

She smothered a sigh and got up from the desk chair to throw away her container. The room was small enough that Chase could sit on one of the beds and still reach to eat off the desk too.

Leesa noticed he was done also. "I'll take that."

He grinned. "Thanks."

Eating together. Cleaning up after him. Spending the night. Almost like a real couple. She glanced at the beds again, then dragged her gaze away.

The two containers more than filled the tiny trashcan and Leesa was considering taking them outside to the dumpster when she realized she probably shouldn't be wandering around outside in the open with Jerry's guys after her. If they could find her in this tiny town they were more talented than she thought, but still, better safe than sorry. She never thought they'd find her at the casino either and look what had happened.

Leesa peeked out the room's curtains one more time, just to make sure. When she turned back she noticed Chase watching her closely.

"Anything good happening outside?"

"Uh, no. Same old stuff. Dumpster. Your truck. The moon." She shrugged and tried to look normal.

He nodded. "Good to know."

Chase rose from his seat on the edge of the bed and walked toward her. With one finger, he moved the curtains slightly and took a look himself. She'd checked enough times herself that she knew he'd see the parking area and the woods beyond. At least she hoped that was all he saw. If a big black car with three guys with guns pulled up, they'd be hard pressed to get out the door without being seen.

She'd have to check out the bathroom window. If it was big enough she could slip out— Chase's hand on her arm broke into her plans. Leesa glanced up at him.

"You know you can tell me anything." His face was near

enough to hers that she couldn't avoid his stare.

"Okay."

Chase shook his head, looking frustrated. "No, don't say okay and then stay all closed up on me. I'm serious."

Leesa nodded. "Okay."

He let out a sigh. "Maybe if I try guessing what's wrong, you'll tell me if I'm warm or cold."

"Nothing's wrong—"

"Then why have you been checking the parking lot since we got here?" Chase cut her off. "My truck is insured and I don't think this is a real high-crime neighborhood if that's what you're worried about."

His tone was gentle but she felt the frustration radiating off him. "Sorry."

He squeezed his eyes shut for a few seconds then came back at her with renewed energy. "Is it a relationship you're running from? An ex? An abusive boyfriend?"

"Chase, no. Stop."

"Bill collectors?"

"No." She laughed at that one. They would probably follow soon if she couldn't figure out how to pay her bills without tipping off Jerry as to where she was hiding.

"Then what?"

"Nothing."

He stood silently and looking unhappy for a moment. "Okay."

Leesa waited to see if he was really giving up or just regrouping for another onslaught of questions. What he did instead took her by surprise. His hand came up and touched her face. His thumb gently brushed her lower lip. Her eyes nearly drifted closed from the sensation.

"I'm here when you need me." His voice was as tender as his touch.

Then in the room that smelled faintly of barbecue sauce and old cigarette smoke, Chase leaned down and kissed her softly. She didn't want soft. Something inside her snapped and she needed hard. She wanted more.

Leesa balled his shirt up in her fists and her mouth became demanding against his. She pushed him toward the nearest bed until the back of his knees hit the edge and buckled. They tumbled as one onto the ugly hotel comforter.

If she surprised him, he didn't let on. His hands tangled in her hair. He angled his head and kissed her deeper as his tongue plunged into her mouth. She ended up straddling him, pawing at the buttons on his shirt as he yanked her sweatshirt up. They broke the kiss long enough for him to pull the item over her head. He flung it to the side.

Their mouths crashed together again in an attempt to satisfy the need that had been building between them all day.

She yanked his shirt from where it had been tightly tucked into his belt, while his hands worked their way up her back beneath her T-shirt. She felt her bra release and moaned. He echoed the sound as her shirt went flying in the same direction her sweatshirt had.

Chase wasn't so shy after all and she liked it. He was hard against her jean-covered thigh. She released his belt for the second time since she'd known him and undid his pants. She felt again the hard, silky length of him. She wanted to feel it so many other places than just her hand.

His eyes closed as she released him from his boxer shorts. Breathless, he panted beneath her. "My boots."

She glanced down and realized he'd be trapped in his jeans

until they took his boots off. She wanted to see every inch of him. It was going to be something worth seeing from the glimpses she'd gotten already.

Topless but still in her own jeans, Leesa crawled off him. She'd never undressed a man completely before, but she supposed it was a lot like doing a striptease, only on him instead of herself. Of course, that didn't mean she couldn't strip too. While watching the hungry expression on his face, she ran her fingers down her body. His eyes remained focused on the motion as she unbuttoned her pants, then slid the zipper down slowly.

She managed to toe off her sneakers while swaying her hips, easing her jeans down ever so slowly. Chase swallowed hard, licking his lips like she'd seen him do before, but this time, the expression on his face was different. Unlike when he was on stage and she could sense his nerves and uncertainty, tonight he looked like a man who knew exactly what was going to happen, and he liked it.

Leesa stepped out of her jeans and swayed before him in nothing but thong underwear. She turned around and let him watch her from behind as she slid those off too. That was it. No high heels, no garters or costume, no makeup or stage lights. Just her, naked before him. She turned to see what he thought of her without all the show biz magic. As his gaze swept her body, pausing at her waxed bikini area, his expression told her he liked it just fine.

He sat up and moved toward her. She held her hand up to stop him. "No not yet. Now it's your turn."

His eyebrows rose, but he leaned back on his elbows on the bed.

Kneeling below him, Leesa took one foot in her hand. She slid his boot off slowly, taking the sock with it. She had no intention of making love to a man wearing socks. His cowboy hat he could wear, if he wanted to. Hell, maybe she would wear it as she rode him.

She shocked herself at that thought. How easy it was to be with him. Natural. Hot.

Her core seemed to be warming the rest of her body from the inside out. The other boot and sock followed the first and not so slowly this time. Then she crawled up his legs, touching as much of him as she could while she worked her way to the waist of his jeans.

Thanks to his rather large erection and very thin boxers equipped with the usual open fly, he was mostly exposed already, but she wanted the jeans gone. The boxers too.

He lifted his pelvis to help her as she wiggled his jeans over his narrow hips and down what proved to be pretty impressively muscular thighs.

When she slid back up his body to retrieve the boxers, he raised his hips again and she couldn't resist what was so close to her face. One flick of her tongue against the tip of him had Chase drawing in a sharp hiss of breath. Happy with that reaction, she pulled the boxers quickly down and went back to taste the entire length of him.

It was so smooth and satiny, she couldn't help running her tongue up one side and down the next, before testing the size out for herself. He was impressive. More than a mouthful.

Her sampling had him grasping at the bedspread. "Leesa."

"Mmm, hmm?" She couldn't say much more with her mouth as full as it was.

"I don't want to finish like this." He hissed in another breath as her hand cupped his balls.

She broke away long enough to say, "Don't worry. We have

all night."

"Oh God." His whole body seemed to shudder beneath her at the thought.

She'd never felt so powerful over a man before. He was at her mercy. She could give him all the pleasure in the world, or withhold it. He would let her. She was certain of that. But there was no way she was going to test that theory. Not tonight. She may tease him in other ways though. She had a feeling he was going to be really fun to tease.

"Mmm." She moaned around his cock and felt it jump in her mouth.

Sweet, innocent Chase who insisted he'd been around the block. Leesa bet she could rattle him if she tried hard enough.

She wet her finger and slid it up and down his slit. He drew in a shuddering breath and bent one knee. She smiled then ran her tongue back to follow where her finger had played.

He remained perfectly still and silent. Waiting? She wouldn't make him wait long. She wet her finger again and began circling the head.

He drew in a sharp breath but again, didn't move. Using both hands and mouth, she massaged him more firmly and continued teasing him.

With his eyes squeezed closed, he couldn't see her, but she had the liberty of watching him. Every expression to cross his face as he reacted to every change in her touch. If he was willing to play, she was happy to oblige. Taking his cock into her mouth again, she slid it slowly in and out of her mouth while her fingers explored his balls and the sensitive spot just behind them.

His body reacted for her. She began to work his cock harder. His breathing quickened and she tasted the precome.

She stroked him until he grabbed at the mattress as his hips thrust forward. He came in her mouth with a loud groan totally opposite of the silent completion he'd had at the club. Unlike at the club when he'd calmly cleaned up and started a conversation with her after he was finished, this time was totally different. After he was done and the final throbbing was over, he reached down and grabbed her. With what could only be called a growl, he flipped them so their positions were reversed and it was Leesa lying back against the bed with Chase between her legs.

"I've wanted to do this since the first time I saw you." That was it for the conversation as he spread her thighs and assaulted her with his tongue.

She shuddered from the first touch of his mouth against her clit. He hadn't lied. This kid knew exactly what he was doing with a woman's body. Leesa decided she better stop calling him a kid. That was the last rational thought she managed because his fingers were inside her pressing something that had her hips lifting off the bed.

She was panting and barely able to swallow away the dryness in her throat by the time her body coiled and poised on the brink of orgasm. That's when he doubled his efforts, sucking on her core while stroking her inside with his fingers until she cried out, bucking beneath him.

It was pleasure so intense it bordered on pain, and yet it kept going for what seemed like forever. She wondered if she could keep coming as long as he kept at it, then wondered if a person could die from orgasms. When she thought she'd reached the pinnacle, she peaked higher until her body released again and she felt warmth flood out of her.

He groaned, sucking her harder.

Finally the spasms slowed. She grabbed his head and

physically pushed him away. "I can't take anymore."

His eyes weren't focused when he looked at her. "Oh my God. That was amazing."

She tried to laugh and found she didn't have the breath or the strength in her stomach muscles to do it. "I know."

He rose and kneeled over her, panting. One glance told her he was hard and ready again. "I want to be inside you."

Leesa swallowed hard. "Yes."

The expression of sheer gratitude on his face would have had her laughing again if she wasn't still out of breath.

Chase dove for his jeans on the floor. He flung cards and cash out of the folds of his wallet before emerging victorious with not one but two condoms. She saw his hands were shaking when he tore one open and slid it over himself. When he braced above her, she looked into his eyes and her fantasy from the club was here, live and in person, staring back into her eyes.

"I think I'm nervous." He laughed shyly and she realized he was trembling from nerves, not exhaustion.

"Don't be." She reached down and grabbed those butt cheeks she'd snuck peeks at in his jeans.

He lay between her thighs. She pulled him closer until he nudged against her entrance. As his eyes never broke from hers, she guided him inside. He slid in easily and filled her like they were made for each other. He laced his fingers with hers. She felt the band on his finger, remembered the ring on her own and was filled with a sense of wonder. She was married to this man, but she couldn't keep him.

That realization filled her eyes with tears. He kissed her mouth, then each of her eyelids. She squeezed them shut to contain the tears. Then need took over again as he stroked inside her slowly. Her hands moved to clutch his back. His reached beneath her and raised her hips off the bed. The speed increased and so did the tension inside her. It could have been minutes, or an hour, she didn't know. Time lost meaning while he loved her, but eventually she shattered around him and he followed shortly after.

Still panting, he rolled off her and onto the pillow. He gathered her in his arms so her head rested against his chest. She could hear his heart still pounding fast.

"Leesa?" His voice vibrated through her ear pressed against him.

"Yeah?"

"Could you maybe not take one of the sleepwalking pills tonight? I really don't want to wake up in the morning and find you've wandered out onto the highway."

She hadn't planned on it anyway. It was stupid to have taken it last night. She had to be on alert in case Bruno had followed them somehow. Even with that worry nagging at her, she couldn't help but smile at Chase's request. "Okay."

He let out a big, contented-sounding sigh. "Good. Thanks."

Then his breathing became deep and steady and she knew the man who was temporarily her husband was asleep.

Chapter Eleven

Chase was barely able to drive the next morning. He kept remembering the incredible night he'd spent with Leesa. He also found it impossible to keep the grin off his face every time he thought about it, which was pretty much every thirty seconds or so.

He glanced across the truck at her now and felt the smile overtake him again.

She caught him looking at her and laughed. "Stop."

"Stop what?" He somehow managed a frown through the grin.

"Fantasizing. You're going to run off the road." Leesa shook her head at him.

Shit. He'd been caught. "How do you know I'm fantasizing?"

"I can just tell."

Hmm. She could already read his mind. They were becoming more and more like a real married couple with every moment they spent together. Chase was about to comment on that when his cell phone rang. He glanced at it in the console, then worked hard to ignore the noise.

"Aren't you going to answer it?"

"Nope. It's Garret."

"I thought he was your friend. Don't you want to talk to

him?"

"Not really." He felt guilty. Garret was his best friend, which meant the minute Chase talked to him, Garret would know something was up. Then he'd have to admit he couldn't remember getting married. Nope. Better to avoid the entire thing for a little while.

"What if it's an emergency?"

Chase considered that. They weren't riding right now so it wouldn't be that he or one of the guys was hurt. If someone had ended up in jail, they'd call one of the guys closer to bail them out. No, most likely Garret wanted to ask about Leesa or brag about whatever he'd done the other night with whatever girl *du jour* he'd picked up. "He'd leave a voicemail or text me if it was important."

Her brow rose at that. "Okay. You know best."

Hmm. Was this wifely nagging? Chase kind of liked it. He smiled again and decided when they stopped for lunch today they should find someplace with a convenience store nearby. After the sex they'd had last night, he was planning on stocking up on lots of condoms.

"What have you told your parents about our marriage?" Her question came from out of the blue.

"Nothing yet. I figure after I get home we can explain everything then go see my uncle."

"You didn't tell them you were bringing me home with you? Oh, Chase. You need to."

Chase glanced over and saw the doubt written all over her face. "Nah. It'll be fine."

"No. You can't just spring this on them."

"I told them I was bringing home a surprise. They won't care. My mama always cooks enough for a dozen people. Our house was the place where everybody always came to hang out. Don't worry."

"What do you think is going to happen when I get out of the truck and they notice our rings, which by the way, I think we should probably stop wearing."

"Why?"

"Because we're getting divorced."

He liked the feel of it around his finger. He didn't want to take it off yet. It made it feel like she belonged to him. Not in a bad way, like some crazy possessive husband or anything. In the way that meant they were in it together, no matter what happened. Partners. He'd be there for her, and she'd be there for him.

"We're still married now."

She let out a laugh. "I still would have had sex with you even if we had taken our rings off. If that's what your worry is."

"You would have?"

"Yes."

"What about tonight?"

She let out another laugh. "In your parents' house? After they know we're not really married?"

"We are really married. We just don't remember getting married," he corrected her.

"Still. You know what I mean."

That put a whole new spin on things. He'd been planning on his parents letting them stay together in his room. He was twenty-two and they were technically and legally married. But the fact they were going to end it shortly might make it a moral grey area for his parents.

"There's always the barn." He raised a brow and shot her a sideways glance. She didn't look entirely happy with that suggestion. "You think about it."

"And you call your parents the next time we stop and tell them what's happening."

Since she had that tone that told him he better do what she asked or else any potential sex in his future was at stake, he nodded. "I will. Promise."

For a new bride, Leesa was sure good at the wife thing.

Chase wanted to do as he promised, if only to show her how amenable he was. The next exit he saw, he pulled the truck off the ramp. He found an empty parking lot and drove in, pulling around the side of the building so the sun wouldn't be in their eyes. It was still early and the bar obviously wasn't open yet so they wouldn't be disturbing anyone by sitting there for a few minutes. He threw the gearshift into park and then dialed his parents, all while Leesa sat in the passenger seat watching and listening.

His mother picked up on the third ring. "Hey, Mama."

"Chase. When will you be home?" He could feel how excited she was to have him coming home for a while. He spent too much time on the road.

"By dinner tonight. Listen I have something to tell you and Daddy. Is he around?"

"He's working. Is everything all right?"

"Yeah, everything is fine. It's just that I kind of did something while I was in Las Vegas." He shot Leesa a look and wished she wasn't listening to his side of the conversation quite so closely.

There was what seemed like a very long pause. "Okay..."

"Um, I kind of got married." He heard his mother's intake of breath and rushed on. "She's very nice and I really like her, but we don't know each other well enough to be married so we're going to see about getting a divorce and I was hoping Uncle Gary can help us."

"Us? She's with you then?"

"Yes." He held his breath waiting for her reaction to that answer.

There was another ominous pause. "Okay. I'll set up the cot in your brother's room. You can bunk with him and she can stay in your room."

"Yes, ma'am."

"I'll see you tonight. Call when you're close."

"I will. Love you."

"Love you too." Then his mother disconnected.

Chase lowered the phone from his face and then flipped it closed. "Um, she was fine with it."

Leesa let out a doubt-filled burst of air. Her expression clearly said, I told you so. "I could hear her, Chase."

"Um, so then you know you should be thinking more about what I said about the barn."

Damn. He was still buying more condoms. He wouldn't have Leesa legally obligated to be around him for long, and he intended on winning her over while he still had her. Whatever it took. Flowers. Dinner. Orgasms. He was willing to try anything at his disposal.

Leesa was watching him again. "So, you really like me?"

"I do." He reached over and pulled her closer. Then kissed her hard to remind her exactly what she'd be missing in that bedroom all alone.

She pulled away after just a few seconds. "Your mother already hates me."

"What? She does not."

Leesa cocked a brow. "She didn't sound happy."

"That's because she was surprised."

"Exactly my point. Imagine if you hadn't called and just showed up with me."

He saw Leesa's eyes getting shiny. "Hey. Do not worry. They will love you. I promise."

"Don't tell them I'm a stripper. Please."

She looked ready to lose it at any second. "Okay. If that's what you want, I won't. I'll tell them you work at one of the clubs serving customers." That wasn't really a lie.

She nodded but still looked near tears. He pulled her closer and hugged her tight.

"Stripping wasn't exactly my life's ambition when I was growing up." Her words were muffled against his chest.

Chase ran his hand up and down her arm, hoping to comfort her. "What was? What did you want to be when you grew up?"

"When I was little? A ballerina. But when I knew better, I was going to school to be a CPA...a certified public accountant."

He rolled his eyes. "I know what a CPA is."

"Sorry." She sniffled and he felt bad immediately.

"It's okay. So why didn't you? Become a CPA, I mean? Besides the fact that to me, stripping sounds a hell of a lot more fun than sitting behind a desk crunching numbers all day, every day."

She lifted her head and looked at him in shock. "You really think that? That stripping is a better job than being an accountant?"

"Sure. I mean it looks fun. The music. All the people. The costumes." He shrugged. "You have your days free. The money is probably pretty good. All the girls look like they enjoy the dancing."

"And it doesn't make you think less of me?"

"Because you're an exotic dancer? Hell no. Why would I?"

He watched her react to that before she grabbed his face and kissed him hard.

When she finally released him, he asked, "Wow, not that I'm complaining, but what was that for?"

"For being so sw—"

"If you call me sweet, I'm afraid I'm going to have to do something nasty to you. Nasty in a good way, of course." He grinned, but his eyes dropped down her body as if considering what he'd like to do.

"What's wrong with being sweet?"

"I don't want you to think of me as sweet. I want to be, I don't know, dangerous."

He traced a path down her throat with his tongue, hoping to prove that if he was willing to seduce her in broad daylight in an abandoned parking lot he was not sweet.

"You ride bulls. That's dangerous." Her voice sounded dreamy, as if she was having trouble maintaining her train of thought. He moved to nibble on her ear.

"Mmm hmm. It is. You better make love to me now just in case I don't make it through next season." His hands wrapped around her hips and he lifted her easily into his lap. Even with them both clothed, he knew he could drive her crazy by rocking her against the bulge in his pants, like he'd done at the club.

She began to breathe harder, and he had a feeling it wouldn't take too much to persuade her to be naughty right here.

"Can I ask you a question?" Chase didn't know why he was still thinking instead of just feeling, but he let curiosity get the best of him.

"You want to ask me something now?" She laughed but continued to press her core against the now throbbing bulge straining against the zipper of his jeans.

He grinned. "It's sex related."

"Oh, well then it's okay."

"What's the naughtiest thing you've ever done?" She didn't immediately answer his question. He felt her stiffen in his lap, so he back pedaled. "You don't have to answer if you don't want to."

She had stopped grinding against him and he regretted asking her anything at all.

"No, it's okay. Probably what I did with you in the back room at the club."

He frowned thinking what she'd done to him the night before was much naughtier than that. "A hand job is the naughtiest thing? I find that very hard to believe."

"It's not what I did that made it bad, but because I didn't know you, and I, you know, took your money." She looked miserable and he didn't feel much better.

He turned serious. "That tip I gave you was for the entire night. For my birthday show on stage, and the dance in the back. I didn't give that to you because of what we did. I had kind of assumed that happened because you were attracted to me."

Her eyes got misty. "It did. I was attracted to you. I am. There's no way I would have done that if I hadn't been attracted to you, Chase."

He considered her reaction to this conversation. "Was that why you said no to the date? Because you thought I was trying to pay you for sex?"

"Yeah." Leesa swallowed hard.

"I told you that night it was a tip."

"Which in my world is kind of code for you do something for me and I'll give you cash."

"I'm sorry. I didn't know."

She shrugged tearfully, acting like it didn't matter though he knew it did. "It's okay. Why did you ask me that? About the naughtiest thing?"

"Because I was hoping having sex in my truck right here, right now, wasn't out of the realm of possibilities." Especially now that he knew what their sleeping arrangements were going to be once they reached his parents' house.

He coaxed her hips forward again and she laughed.

"I'm in jeans."

"Mmm. If you were going to stay my wife, I'd buy you a different dress for every day of the week. That way when I decided I couldn't live another moment without making love to you, I could just pull over and set you in my lap." He frowned. "Does that sound sick and perverted?"

She shook her head. "No. It sounds sweet."

When she leaned in and kissed him, he decided he didn't mind being called sweet as long as it was followed by a deep soul-filled kiss.

Leesa pulled back. "Drive this thing farther around the back of the building and I'll consider it."

His eyes flew open. She was serious, and he was seriously hard. He set her firmly but gently back into the passenger seat and threw the truck into reverse. "No problem."

Chapter Twelve

"Mama. Daddy. This is Leesa Santiago."

Chase's father took a step forward, his hand extended. His mother stood a step back, wringing her hands. Her mouth pursed tightly, she was definitely sizing Leesa up and deciding exactly how large a disaster it was that her son was married to her.

"Ma'am. Sir." Leesa shook her father-in-law's hand, nodded once to her mother-in-law, and took a step back into her imaginary safety zone. Chase's hand settled on the small of her back and she felt instantly better. His show of support didn't go unnoticed judging by how both parent's eyes zoomed in directly on the action.

"I think we should sit down and discuss this." Chase's father spun for the front door of the house.

"Before dinner?" His mother turned toward her husband.

"Yes, Martha. Before dinner." He sent his wife a stern look that Leesa could never ever imagine crossing Chase's face, and she had to wonder how he could have been birthed from this couple. With his constant grin and sunny disposition, they couldn't be more different.

"Uh oh." Leesa whispered barely loud enough for Chase to hear.

He took her hand and squeezed it. "Don't worry. It'll be fine."

She nodded, not believing him one bit. Somehow facing his parents was nearly as frightening as seeing Bruno and the hit men in the casino had been. Chase pulled her toward the door that his parents had just disappeared through.

"I didn't know you knew my last name." It was a ridiculous thing to say, but his knowing her full name intrigued her.

"It was on the marriage certificate," he answered her softly while holding open the door for her to walk through.

"Oh yeah." She had a feeling that little piece of paper was about to get both of them a lecture.

He held her more tightly and she was glad for it as they entered the kitchen and saw both parents already seated at the far side of the table, facing them, like a board of inquisitors.

Chase released his hold to pull the chair out. She missed his touch immediately as she sat, and he took the seat next to her. Thankfully, once he was settled, he reached out again, placing their joined hands on the table, and covering them both with his left hand so his wedding band was front and center.

Two sets of eyes dropped to stare at what Leesa had no doubt Chase had done on purpose.

"So, Miss Santiago. Or should I call you Mrs. Reese?" Chase's father focused his attention on Leesa.

"Um, Leesa will be fine."

"Would you like to tell us how you met our son and ended up married to him?" Mr. Reese's gaze settled pointedly on the gold rings on their joined hands once again.

Leesa opened her mouth but found Chase's mother had jumped in. "It's just too soon. How long have you known each other? This is the first time we've met her, Chase."

"Mama. We're not arguing with you. We know we need to undo this. I just need Uncle Gary to help us with the legal stuff."

"Then why did you do it in the first place, Chase?" His father's tone clearly showed his disappointment with his son.

"I don't know how it happened, Daddy." He faced his father with the truth.

"You just woke up to find yourselves married?"

"Yes."

His father quickly recovered from the shock of that revelation as a look of realization crossed his face. "Were you drinking?"

Chase nodded solemnly. "Yes, sir. I was."

He'd left her part in it out. She didn't volunteer the information that she'd drugged herself with over-the-counter pain medication/sleeping pills. At this point, what would it have helped?

"Gary's away in the next county for a big trial. He won't be back until next week. I'll call him and tell him about the...situation." His father's face said everything else his words didn't.

"Thank you." Chase drew in a deep breath and turned to Leesa. He forced a smile. "I guess we're married for another week. That okay with you?"

She nodded. Actually, she wasn't looking forward to leaving him when the time came.

"These things don't get fixed overnight, Chase. Maybe you can file for divorce next week, but it could take at least thirty days, if not months to be finalized. I'm not sure about the laws, but marriage isn't like turning on and off a light switch. It's serious. It's a legally binding contract that shouldn't be entered into lightly."

"Of course. You're right. I wasn't thinking the timing of the legalities through." Chase glanced at her. "Is that going to be all right?"

She squeezed his hand this time. "It's okay. However long it takes is fine."

"What about your job?" He kept his voice low, as if speaking only to her.

"I'm done with that job. I was going to look for something else."

"Really?" He looked like he wanted to talk more, but instead he glanced to his parents. This was a conversation for when they were alone. He knew she didn't want his parents to know what she did for a living. "Um, we've been on the road all day. If it's all right, I'd like to get Leesa settled in her room in case she wants to clean up before dinner."

He got a nod from his father and thankfully, they were dismissed.

Chase carried his duffle bag filled with his clothes—or more accurately his dirty laundry—into his brother's bedroom and let it drop heavily to the floor.

His older brother, Cody, glanced up from where he lay on the bed. He pulled an ear bud from one ear and gave the bag a pointed look. "Um, hello. Welcome back."

"Yeah. Thanks." Chase could hear Cody's music coming through the tiny earpiece. The pounding bass sounded like one of the heavy metal bands his brother liked to listen to.

Cody shoved a piece of notebook paper into the book open in his lap and flipped the cover of the thick textbook closed.

135

"First off, what's wrong? And second, um, why are you and your bag in my room? Besides just saying hello to me, I mean."

Chase let out snort. "I'm sleeping in here with you for a while."

Pointedly looking at the one and only bed in the room, which was a double but barely big enough to contain Cody's six-foot-plus frame, Cody raised a brow. "Okay. What's wrong with your room?"

Chase kicked at the carpet with the toe of his boot. His older brother was not going to let him get away with coming home from Vegas married. If he thought telling Garret and the guys was going to be bad, telling Cody would be far worse. "Um, somebody's staying in there for a little bit. Don't worry. I'm not sharing your bed. Mama was supposed to bring in the cot."

She'd probably been too upset and forgotten.

Procrastinating telling wasn't going to do any good. Cody would meet Leesa at dinner, and best to get the explanations out of the way now and in private rather than at the dinner table with his parents who had already raked them both over the coals.

"Who's staying here for awhile?" Cody wasn't stupid. Hell, he was the brain in the family. While Chase had decided to make a living out of hanging on the back of a bull to the eight second buzzer, Cody was in veterinary school, dedicating himself to learning how to keep animals healthy. Their joint skills, Chase's experience with their temperament and Cody's expertise with the medical aspect, would go a long way to taking their father's farm from a two-bit steer ranch, to a bucking bull stock breeder to be reckoned with. That way, when the time came that Chase couldn't ride anymore, his future was secured in doing work he loved.

Hopefully that time was a long way away. Hell, it would be

ten, fifteen years before he retired. God willing.

"Chase?"

He hadn't answered his brother's question, but he had to. "It's my wife. She's staying in my room."

Cody's brow rose slightly. "Your wife?" He laughed and swung his feet to the floor as he sat on the edge of the mattress. "Well then, I guess that brings up a whole new line of questioning now doesn't it."

Line of questioning. "I thought you're studying to be a vet, not a lawyer."

"Ha, joke all you want, but I'm thinking you bringing home a wife that Mama and Daddy never met and never even heard of isn't going over too well. I guess I can just wait for the yelling and find out then."

Chase let out a huff of air. "We already got our dressing down the minute we walked through the door."

"Okay. So then it should be easier telling me, since you broke the ice and practiced on them."

Chase drew in a deep steadying breath and dragged the chair out from beneath the desk. He straddled it backward and began the story. He and Cody were close. Always had been. It wasn't until Chase started spending more time away from home, and Cody was too busy studying to come out on the road with him much, that they had started to drift a bit.

But the bond of brotherhood didn't fade with time or distance and Cody was still the guy Chase asked advice of for everything. Chase had talked to Cody before he first did it with his girlfriend in high school after the prom. It was Cody who took him out for a beer, illegally since he was still underage then, after the girl he was seeing in college broke his heart.

Out of respect for Leesa, he skipped over most of the strip

club details. "I was out with the guys for my birthday. I met her two nights ago at a club in Vegas."

He should have known Cody was too quick to leave out much. His eyes opened wide. "Oh my God, she's a stripper."

"Shhh!" Chase glanced at the open door, then thought better and got up to close it. "You can't tell Mama or Daddy."

Cody shook his head. "Man, when you mess up, you really do it big."

"Shut up. It's not like that. She's not like that."

"Then tell me how it is." Cody leaned forward and waited.

Chase waited for Cody to comment further with some smart-ass statement, but he didn't. He was in older brother mode which would mean a certain amount of teasing was to be expected, but still, he was giving Chase a chance to explain. If only his parents had, not that he could explain what he was about to tell Cody to them.

Shaking his head, the facts began to seep out, more than he'd intended but he needed Cody to understand how he felt and why. "From the moment I saw her. I swear, it was like I'd gotten knocked in the head. You know right before you pass out and your vision narrows down to just a tunnel in front of you?"

"No, not really and you've been hit in the head too many times and I think you should get a CT scan before you leave here, but go on."

"Anyway, I only saw her. We were in a packed club, my friends were all there. There was music and shouting and lights and all these people, but I only saw her." He leaned back in the seat and adjusted the brim of his hat. "I don't know. I've wanted girls before, but not like this."

"So it was sexual."

"No. I mean, yeah. Of course that too. The sex is..." Chase

cleared his throat. It felt strange talking about sex with his wife to his brother, but this whole situation was a bit out of the ordinary. "It's so much more than that. I want to know everything about her. I want to, hell I don't know, see her baby pictures. And watch her while she's watching her favorite movie. See her wake up and smile at me every morning."

Cody was watching him closely. "So it's love?"

Chase wasn't afraid of that word the way some men were, but he also wasn't one to use it lightly. "I don't know. All I know is that I want to find out if it is. And if I don't give us a chance to find out, I'm afraid it's something I'll regret the rest of my life."

"Okay, so let me get this straight. You married the girl to keep her from getting away so you could decide if you love her or not?"

"No, getting married was kind of an accident."

"How do you accidentally get married?"

"You have a few too many beers and shots of bourbon and wake up in Vegas with a wedding band." Chase shook his head. "I know. Only me."

Cody laughed. "No actually I think that happens quite a lot in Vegas. Mix bars open twenty-four hours a day with no-waiting wedding chapels and I can only imagine. I think what is typically you is staying married after you get drunk and married."

"We're not staying married. We're waiting for Uncle Gary to get back from some big case he's working on so he can help us." Chase's heart twisted at the thought of how soon that day may be.

"Ah. So how did Mama and Daddy take it?"

"It could have been better. I gotta ask you a favor. I didn't tell them what she does for a living."

Cody raised a brow. "You lied?"

"No, I avoided telling the truth, which I tried to do with you but you guessed."

"They didn't take one look at her and know? And what is her name, anyway? This new soon-to-be-ex sister-in-law of mine."

"Leesa. No, they didn't know. She's not like that."

"Okay. If you say so."

Chase knew Cody was picturing high hair and gold sequined tube tops. Meanwhile, if he got Leesa to wear anything besides that oversized sweatshirt he'd seen her in over the two days they'd been together, it would be a good day.

There was a soft knock on the bedroom door and Chase frowned at Cody. "Expecting company?"

"No, but today's been chock full of surprises so who the hell knows." He shrugged.

Chase rose and opened the door to find Leesa, looking so lost and out of place his heart broke. Reaching out, he took her hand and pulled her into the room. "Hey. How'd you find me?"

She shot a quick look at Cody before focusing back on him. "Your sister, I guess. I was coming out of the bathroom when she ran past in the hallway. I asked her where you were and she pointed at this door."

"I'm sorry. I should have introduced you to Christine. Yeah, she's our sister, and she's ten, so I'm guessing one of her favorite shows was coming on television and she couldn't stop long enough to be polite. And while you're meeting family..." Chase realized that for now at least, they were her family too. "This is Cody. He's my older brother."

"Older, smarter and better-looking brother you mean."

Cody delivered Leesa the smile that had won him homecoming king and countless girlfriends during high school. He rose and extended a hand to her. She shook it and mumbled a hello, then she was glancing back at Chase.

"What's up?" He put a hand around her waist and rubbed her back, something he found himself doing a lot lately. He couldn't seem to be near her and not touch her. Especially now that they'd had sex. She was like a magnet and he was a giant hunk of metal.

"I didn't know what I should wear for dinner."

Cody laughed. "What you have on is fine."

"Really? It's a sweatshirt."

"Really. It's fine. We're not formal around here."

"Okay. Good, because I don't have much with me."

"Don't worry." He planned on remedying that situation tomorrow. If she wouldn't let him buy her clothes, he'd buy them on his own and surprise her, and then throw away the receipt so she had to accept them.

"Okay. Thanks. I think I'm going to go lay down for a bit before dinner." She looked pretty tired, which wasn't a surprise.

Chase's mind shot back to what they'd done for most of the night instead of sleep and his body reacted to it immediately. He couldn't help himself. He leaned down and kissed her. "Okay. I'll come get you when it's time to eat."

She nodded. "Nice meeting you."

Cody nodded back. "You too."

Then she was gone. Chase watched her walk down the hall until she disappeared into his bedroom and then closed the door.

When he turned back to his brother, he noticed Cody smiling and shaking his head. "Oh, man."

Chase frowned. "What?"

"You got it bad."

Chase swallowed hard, but didn't deny it.

"And on top of that, I'm not going to worry about you being in here too much at night."

"What do you mean?"

"You can't be more than a few inches from her. There is no way you're sleeping in here. I bet the minute Mama and Daddy are asleep you'll be in there with her performing your husbandly duties."

"Shut up." Chase scowled at his brother's coarseness.

"What? You're allowed."

"Mama and Daddy don't think so and it's their house."

Cody shook his head. "Yeah, I bet they don't think you're allowed. Man, she's pretty though."

Chase sat again. "She is, isn't she? I mean, it's not just me, right? The more I get to know her, the more beautiful she gets."

Cody shook his head. "Oh boy. There is no way you're getting a divorce."

"I have to. We knew each other for like twenty-four hours before. Nobody stays married after that. Do they?"

"I don't know, but if anybody can make it work, it'll be you."

Chase drew in a long breath. "I don't know if she wants to stay married."

"Have you asked her?"

"No."

"Well, maybe you should."

Chase considered that. "I want to give her a few days."

"A few days to what? Get used to the glowing reception

from her in-laws?"

"I was thinking maybe she'd get used to, you know, me."
Chase felt his face get hot remembering the sex. Damn, was he
blushing?

Cody eyes opened wide. "That good, huh?"

"I can't believe I'm talking to you about this, but oh yeah.
Like...yeah." Chase couldn't form the words to express how
great it was, which was probably for the best because he was
sure Leesa wouldn't appreciate him talking about her that way
to his brother. But even saying it out loud made him more
determined to find a way to win her heart.

Chapter Thirteen

Leesa had never thought she'd feel safe again, but she felt moderately safe at Chase's family farm. Sure, Bruno could find her here. The scenario kept running through her head during the drive from Nevada to Oklahoma. How they might have seen her getting into Chase's truck, if not live and in person then maybe by reviewing the security tapes from the parking garage. Then they could have run Chase's license plate and found out his address and been waiting here for them.

Arriving and finding his family hadn't been taken hostage at gunpoint by three of Jerry's men had helped her confidence a bit. Sleeping an entire night and waking up the next day still alive and in Chase's bed helped even more.

Each hour that passed made her think she might actually be in the clear. For now. That didn't change the fact once she and Chase signed those papers she still had nowhere to go. Jerry could be watching her family, waiting for her to get home. Then again, maybe she was small potatoes to them. Too much work to bother with.

She drew in a deep shaky breath. Who knew? All she did know was Chase's family couldn't be nicer. Sure, the beginning had been pretty rough, but it seemed they were the forgiving kind. After letting her and Chase know exactly how unhappy they were about their accidental drunken wedding vows, they'd let it go. Surprisingly. Amazingly. Lovingly.

After that initial meeting, his parents had been really nice. His brother seemed to like her, and his sister, when she sat still for more than a minute, did also.

They'd welcomed her into their home, a stranger, and treated her like family, right down to the lecture when she'd arrived. She'd even done the dishes with his mother after dinner. Leesa could see herself here. She didn't dare think the word forever, because she was only here until the mysterious and lawyerly Uncle Gary arrived back from wherever. She tried not to think as far as next week, even though she knew she needed to make a plan. She didn't want to think past right now.

The sun was shining. She was on a farm for the first time in her life, and the man who was her husband—for now—was out there doing some sort of cowboy stuff and Leesa wanted to see it. She didn't have him for long, but she might as well enjoy him while she did have him. Watching him do his thing would be fun.

In sneakers more suited to city life than the country, she tried to tiptoe her way around the mud puddles and made her way to the barn behind the house. She didn't have a clue what she'd find in there. Horses? Cows? Bulls maybe? It would make sense. He rode them. With that in mind, she opened the barn door gingerly, just a crack. What she was thinking, she didn't know. If a bull did come charging at that door and want out, she wouldn't be able to stop him.

What she saw was definitely not a bull. In fact, it wasn't very cowboy-like at all, but that didn't mean she didn't like it.

Swinging the large wooden door wider, Leesa slid through and closed it silently behind her.

"Ten more." Cody stood below Chase, who was hanging by his knees from a metal bar spanning a stall door.

She watched Chase gather his strength—she could actually see him doing it, like he was summoning the energy from somewhere else. He set his jaw, let out a nearly feral growl and pulled his body up again.

"Come on. Nine more."

Chase repeated the move with another groan.

"Good. Eight." Cody counted down, backwards from ten, encouraging his brother with each repetition.

Chase's bare chest and abdominal muscles glistened with sweat in spite of the cool air that made Leesa cross her arms in front of her for warmth. His muscles moved, tensing, flexing, working. She'd seen those muscles flex up close and personal the other night.

Her mouth went dry from the vision. She swallowed hard. Then the counting was done and she realized both Reese men were watching her.

Chase while hanging upside down. His brother, standing next to him, grinning. Grabbing the bar with his hands, Chase swung his legs down and landed with a soft thud on the barn's wooden floor. He was in workout clothes, but seeing him in sweatpants did nothing to diminish her appreciation.

"Hey. Sorry to bother you."

He walked over to her. "No bother at all. But don't worry, because even if you were you can bother me all you want."

"He just wants to get out of the rest of the workout." Cody grinned.

"Yeah, whatever." Chase ran a hand up and down her arm. "You want me to show you around?"

"Sure." Leesa could see it was a barn, no doubt about it, but it looked more like a gym inside and there wasn't an animal in sight.

"When Daddy built the new barn closer to the pasture, I turned this place into a kind of workout room."

"I had no idea you had to be in such good shape to ride bulls."

"He was in better shape when he left here for the start of the last season. Life and debauchery on the road has done in his body. He'll be lucky if I can whip him into shape by the start of next season." Cody crossed his arms in front of himself, as if daring Chase to argue.

"Cody fancies himself my trainer." Chase spoke low, but loud enough so Cody could hear. Brothers teased each other, she supposed. Brothers and sisters, however, did not. At least that was her experience with her older brother growing up.

"Anyway, you need strength, but it's not really pure muscle that keeps you on the bull. It's being able to stay centered, and correct your position when you get off-balance. Yeah, you need strong forearms to stay forward over your rope, and you need strong thigh muscles to bear down on the bull's sides, but the core muscles, the stomach and lower back, those are the most important in bull riding. It's the constant effort to remain centered that gives bull riders the strongest core muscle in professional sports."

There was that passion he always showed when talking about his sport. Leesa attempted to respond appropriately. "Wow. I had no idea."

In her peripheral vision, she saw Cody rolling his eyes and she smiled.

Chase was fascinating. His muscles too were fascinating. Her gaze dropped down to the ones exposed by his lack of shirt. She couldn't see his thighs but she sure remembered them. His back muscles too. She'd felt them flex beneath her fingers while he loved her.

She swallowed. "So you built this in here. It's really nice."

Chase watched her face. If he didn't see the need she was suddenly feeling then she'd be really surprised. His gaze shot to his brother, then back to her. "Thanks. So we have the abs area, which you saw, then I have the punching bag to help my reflexes. We have the free weights. I use those for squats for my legs and also to build my arms and back. There's even a mat on the floor where Cody and I spar a bit. That is mostly for fun, because I like kicking his butt so much, but it also helps with my reaction time."

"Yeah, he wishes he could kick my butt." Cody shook his head.

Chase ignored his brother. "Then there's a practice bull in the back. That's what I started out on when I was young. It's the barrel kind, not a live one, and we're gonna put you up on it while you're here."

"Me?" Her voice came out in a squeak.

"Sure. Don't worry. I'll be gentle with you." He grinned. "In fact, maybe we should wander out back and take a look at that now."

His hand was still running up and down her arm making her wish there was no clothing between them.

She glanced at his brother and saw him shaking his head. "I'm leaving. Daddy's at work, Christine is at school and Mama's at the food store. You two have half an hour alone out here, then I'm coming back and we're finishing this workout."

Chase grinned. "Okay."

Then they were alone and Chase's head was ducking lower towards hers.

"Hey there." His voice was low and sexy as he leaned in closer.

"Hey."

"I missed you last night." His hand rose to brush a hair off her cheek. "I know we only slept together two nights but I kind of got used to you in my bed. I missed it."

"I missed you too." He had no idea how much. She slept much better with him next to her, for so many reasons.

He let out a groan, and before she knew it they were kissing like there was no tomorrow. In reality, after next week, for them, there wasn't. She kissed him back with enough passion to last her for a lifetime because the memories of this time would have to.

"I want you." He spoke against her ear, sending a shiver through her.

"Here? Chase, we can't."

"Sure we can. That's why Cody left us alone. You heard him. We have half an hour alone. I can make it. Don't worry." His ever-present smile was looking devilish again.

"We can't. Can we? Really?" She sure wanted to, but it was broad daylight and they were in his parents' barn.

"Oh yeah, we can." He grinned as his hands moved to her waist.

"What about...you know. Protection."

He was nibbling her ear again and she had trouble coming up with what she'd wanted to say. Luckily the word had come to her. Being on the run was one thing, Being pregnant and in hiding quite another.

She felt him smile against her ear. "I got that covered, so to speak."

"You do? Where?" She glanced at his clothing. He wasn't wearing very much and it didn't look like there was a pocket in those sweats.

Chase wasn't lying. He pulled himself up onto the bar he'd been doing his pull-ups on. Holding himself up one-handed, he reached above his head and felt along the edge of the loft above. When he dropped down to the floor again, he was victoriously holding up a condom.

Leesa frowned. "How—?"

"Wishful thinking on my part. I told you we were going to do it in the barn if my parents wouldn't let us sleep together."

"I didn't think you'd meant it."

His mouth hovered above hers again. She felt his hands on the hem of her sweatshirt. "I never tease about sex."

Her sweatshirt was off, her mouth was covered by Chase's kiss and she had to believe him. They were going to do it right here, right now, in the barn. The way she felt just being near him, it couldn't be soon enough.

Cody returned, as promised, in exactly thirty minutes. Luckily for Chase, he'd been too excited having Leesa in his arms again to last very long. He didn't need any more time than that. That didn't mean he didn't wish they had all night every night together though. Even after the time they'd just spent together inside one of the old stalls, he was still ready to go again.

Now that Leesa had gone back to the house and Cody had returned, Chase supposed he'd have to work off this energy sparring with his brother instead. Not half as much fun, but what could he do?

Cody was grinning and shaking his head as he walked into the barn.

"What?"

"You two. The attraction between you guys is so strong I

could practically see it in the air. Why are you getting divorced again?"

Chase sighed. "I told you. It was way, way too soon."

"Yeah, whatever."

"Are you trying to tell me we should stay married?"

"Yeah, I am. Just because you rushed into the marriage doesn't mean you should rush into the divorce just as quickly."

Drawing in a deep, frustrated breath, Chase sank down onto the weight bench. "I don't get you. You were always the one telling me not to fall in love with the first girl I slept with. Not to date seriously in college. To just have fun and enjoy being single. Now here you are telling me to not get divorced?"

Cody huffed out a laugh. "First of all, you've never listened to me anyway. In fact, you usually do the exact opposite."

"Is that what this is? Reverse psychology?" Chase narrowed his eyes at his brother. Things were confusing enough. He didn't need Cody messing with his head too.

"No, not at all, but you're right, since you probably will do the opposite of what I tell you to, I should have thought of the reverse psychology thing before."

Chase scowled, but his brother continued talking undeterred. "Chase, I'm saying this because anyone can see there is something going on between you two. Maybe you did just meet, and I sure as hell don't believe in love at first sight, but you two have a thing for each other. Maybe it's just sexual but hell, even if it is, why would you want to go and end it so soon? Judging by the look on your face when I walked in here just now, that half hour you were alone with her was pretty damn good."

Chase shook his head. "I truly hate you knowing anything at all about my sex life with Leesa."

Cody laughed. "You didn't used to hate it. You used to rush home from each and every date and tell me every damn detail about you and whoever back in the old days. Even when I covered my head with a pillow and tried to not listen you still insisted on telling me."

He made it sound so cheesy. Chase scowled. "Hey, it's not like I was bragging to you or anything. I wanted your advice. You're the older brother. That's supposed to be what you're good for."

"Exactly. So listen to me now. I've been through all your crushes. It's different with this girl. You don't want me knowing details about you two because you have feelings for her."

Chase considered that, not that he had to. He knew Cody was right. He just really hated to admit it to the know-it-all. He gave in, but only part way. "Maybe."

Cody let out a snort. "Yeah, whatever. Come on. Let's get back to work. You're getting out of shape. You're starting to get a gut on you."

"I am not." Chase frowned down at his stomach. The definition of his ab muscles was still clearly visible.

"Okay, if you say so. Get up. Time for leg work." Cody grinned.

Gut or not, he knew he needed to work out. He always felt good after he did, and it helped his riding so much when he was in top shape. Still, Chase couldn't help but think about what had been nagging him about Leesa for days now.

When he didn't get up from the bench right away, his brother kicked his foot. "Hey. Leg work, lazy."

"She's hiding something from me." Chase rose from the bench and watched Cody pile the weights on the barbell.

"Leesa? What do you mean hiding something? Like what?"

"I don't know. That's the problem. She won't admit anything's wrong, but something is. I can tell."

"How?" Cody put the barbell on Chase's shoulders and stayed behind him with both hands poised to take it from him if necessary.

Chase lowered into a squat, then slowly straightened his legs again. "She won't let me take her out in public. She's a nervous wreck all the time. Always watching the rearview mirror while I'm driving, looking out the window a hundred times the night we spent in a hotel room on the way here. It's like she's waiting for someone to find her, or catch her."

Cody frowned. "Like who?"

Chase was starting to get winded talking. He took in a deep breath and pushed himself for one more repetition before answering. "I don't know. An ex maybe?"

"You think maybe she's running from a bad break up?"

"Yeah, that's what I'm thinking." At least Chase hoped it was an ex and not a current boyfriend, or worse, husband. Would that make them bigamists? His parents would really love that.

"Three more. Have you asked her?" Cody pushed Chase to work harder but didn't let the topic drop.

"No." Chase was down to one-word answers now. It was all he could manage through his clenched teeth. He groaned with the exertion as his muscles burned.

"Don't you think you should, dork?"

"Smart ass." It had taken extra effort to get out the two words instead of just one, but it had been worth it.

Chase hated to admit it, but Cody was right. He had to ask Leesa what was wrong. The question was, why should she tell him? They were joined now, but not for long.

Not for the first time, he hoped his uncle's case ran longer than expected. He could use all the time he could get. Hell, a few more rendezvous in the barn might just do it—convince her to stay with him at least as his girlfriend if not his wife.

He pushed out one more rep as Cody counted it from behind him.

Workout or not, an image flashed through Chase's head. Leesa, flushed and breathless, her hands braced against the wall of the stall. He had been in the perfect position to see her green eyes as she peeked over her shoulder while he loved her. He had watched her face, when he wasn't too enthralled with watching himself slide in and out of her as his hands gripped her perfectly rounded hips.

He wrestled his mind away from the memory before he embarrassed himself in front of his brother.

One last repetition and finally Cody took the barbell from him. "Good job. Next—"

Chase turned to face Cody. "No more. I'm done for today."

"We just got started." His brother looked like he was about to argue, but it wasn't going to work. Chase had his mind set.

"I got something to do."

Understanding flashed across Cody's face. He grinned. "Don't you mean someone to do?"

He shook his head. "Pig."

"Lover boy." Cody grinned broader.

Chase rolled his eyes. Telling Cody anything was a big mistake. He should really learn to keep his mouth shut.

Chapter Fourteen

Leesa ran one finger over the frame. The photo was an action shot of Chase on a bull. He had his hat on, pulled low over his eyes, but she knew it was him, and not just because the picture was on the dresser in his bedroom. She'd know him anywhere now. The way he held himself. The lines of his body.

It was an amazing shot. The photographer had captured the action so well that even frozen on the static picture, the viewer could feel the motion. She could see the power of the bull as all four of its feet left the ground in a giant leap. She could see how Chase had bent at the waist to absorb the shock of the move and keep his seat. The fringe on his chaps stood straight out from his legs, defying gravity, testament to how jarring the animal's move was to the rider on his back.

Her heart hurt thinking of him in that situation, not just once but weekly or more. How long before something bad happened to him? An injury must be inevitable. She finally understood why he'd laughed at her when at the strip club she'd asked if his wrists hurt from the handcuffs. In the truck he'd told her about how guys have ridden with their broken jaws wired shut. Or with backs that had been broken just weeks before. It was frightening. At the same time, looking at the picture and remembering the excitement in his voice as he told her about riding, she could understand his passion for it.

She felt it.

On the wall was a framed newspaper article. *Local Bull Rider Wins Rookie of the Year.* Chase stood in the black and white photo holding a boxed buckle and wearing the wide grin she'd come to know as his. She swallowed hard when she remembered that after she left here she'd likely never see it again.

He'd said his rides were usually televised. Could she bring herself to watch him once she left? She had a feeling she would, and that it would tear a fresh hole in her chest every time she did.

A quick knock on the open door startled her. She turned to find Chase, grin and all. "Get changed. I'm taking you out on a date."

"What?" Leesa immediately felt panic. She felt moderately safe here on his family's farm, but going out into town, that felt like asking for trouble. She scrambled for an excuse that wouldn't sound bogus. "No, I can't. I don't have anything to wear."

She glanced down at the sweatshirt that had become her security blanket over the past few days. Though her constant wearing of it was starting to show. She'd have to ask if she could use the washing machine.

"No worries. I got you covered." Chase brought a shopping bag from behind his back.

Frightened as she was to leave the house, Leesa was still a girl, and all girls love presents. Her curiosity got the better of her. "What's that?"

"Open it." He walked closer and held the bag out.

Eyeing him suspiciously, she took it. From under the tissue paper, she pulled out a navy blue dress with tiny white flowers on it. Holding it up, it looked like it would actually fit her. "How
156

did you know my size?"

He smiled, then shrugged. "I've had my hands on enough parts of you to be able to estimate what size dress you take. Do you think it'll work?"

Her cheeks grew hot at the memory of those hands on her. "Yeah. I do."

"There's a pair of shoes in the bag too."

She raised a brow. "You haven't had your hands on my feet." Or had he?

"No, but I peeked inside your sneakers while you were in the shower back in Vegas and saw what size they were." Chase donned a shy, almost contrite expression.

Leesa laughed. "You did? Why?"

"They looked so tiny sitting there on the floor." He shrugged. "I was curious."

"I suppose this dress is just in case we need to, uh, pull over for any reason?"

His grin lit up his entire face. "You never know."

"You never know." She couldn't help but smile too. She had a feeling he'd stocked up on condoms too while he was out shopping for clothes for her.

"There's also a little white sweater-type thing in the bag too, in case you get cold later."

She glanced down and indeed there was. She supposed he was getting tired of seeing her in the sweatshirt. She guessed she couldn't blame him. "Thank you. You're so sweet. You really shouldn't have bought me anything."

Leesa didn't want him spending money on her when she was going to have to leave and never look back.

Chase dismissed her thanks with a wave of a hand. "It's nothing, and I really mean that. There is one store in town that has women's clothes and the choices are pretty limited. I did the best I could, but we can go to the mall one day. It's about an hour away but there I can buy you something really nice."

"Chase. I don't want you buying me things."

"Why not? I told you, I have money."

Somehow he'd inched closer. He was so close his chest nearly brushed against hers as his face hovered just inches above. She looked up at him now. "I know, but you shouldn't be spending it on me."

"Too bad." He dipped his head lower and captured her lips. The bag was between them. As he kissed her, he managed to take it out of her grasp and drop it onto the bed next to them. She had a feeling he would like to drop her on that bed too, but would never do that with his mother in the house.

He pressed close and kissed her harder until the sound of rushing footsteps in the hall had him pulling away. Christine flew past the door, then stopped and backed up. "Chase. Mama wants to make sure you're not here for dinner before she defrosts the steaks."

Watching her, he waited for her answer.

"Where would we be going?" Leesa knew he could hear the hesitation in her voice.

Chase glanced at her. "Just out in town. It's a tiny little bar that serves food in the side room. It's the middle of the week. We'll probably be one of the few people there. One hour. We'll eat and then I'll bring you right home. Promise."

Leesa drew in a big breath. It was probably safe. Actually, it might be good for her to go. If there had been strangers poking around here asking questions lately, this was a small enough town that word would spread. She was so isolated on the farm she'd never hear it here, but at a bar in town where the locals hung out, she definitely would catch some of the gossip.

She nodded. "Okay."

Chase grinned. "Good." He turned toward his sister. "Tell Mama Leesa and I are going out for dinner."

Christine skittered away down the hall and Leesa felt Chase's gaze back on her.

"Thank you."

She raised a brow. "You're the one taking me out and buying me things. Why are you thanking me?"

"For giving me someone to do those things for." His hand touched her face and as usual, sent warmth straight through her.

She shook her head slowly. "Why hasn't someone already scooped you up and claimed you as their own?"

He shrugged. "I guess I've been waiting to be claimed by the right one."

Her heart twisted. Another time, another place, she would love to be that one. "Get out. I have to change."

"Can't I stay and...help?" The devilish side crept out through his usual angelic aura.

"No." She pushed him backward toward the door.

He went easily enough, grinning. "Can't wait to see you in that dress."

"Yeah, and don't think I don't know why."

Chase didn't argue. He just laughed and began pulling the door shut. "See you in a few minutes."

"Okay."

When the door clicked shut, Leesa turned toward the bag on the bed. Her gaze caught her reflection in the mirror. Her cheeks were flushed, her eyes bright, and her lips just a tad bit swollen from his kisses. If she hadn't already decided not to be, she'd have to say that she looked like a woman in love.

Chase's hometown reminded her a bit of her own as they drove down the main street. He parked along the side of a dark colored building with a sign lit by a few bulbs that read *Murphy's.*

He didn't immediately jump out to run and open the truck door for her, something she'd learned to wait for him to do so he didn't kill himself trying to get around the hood only to find her already out of the vehicle. That was her clue he wanted to say something. "Something wrong?"

"Um, not really. It's just that this is a small town."

She nodded. "Yeah?"

"Everyone here knows me. They have since the day I was born." He looked pained. "I think maybe we should take our rings off before we go inside."

Leesa felt a little twinge in the vicinity of her heart. "Oh. Okay."

Chase grabbed both of her hands before she had a chance to absorb the meaning of what he'd suggested. "Listen to me first. It's not that I'm not proud to have you on my arm, because I am. But if we're gonna end this thing, it will be easier if no one in town knows. The gossips will chew on this forever and I...I don't want that. Do you understand?"

Two things struck Leesa. One was Chase's use of the word if. *If* we're gonna end this thing. The second was the expression on his face, as if it would cause him pain later on to be reminded by town gossip that they'd once been married.

Leesa shook that theory from her mind. She was thinking like a silly girl with a crush, assuming he felt the same way. Chase was young and attractive and in the midst of building a great career. He was in the public eye. He probably had girls hanging all over him all the time. He could be with someone new the minute she was gone.

"Okay. That's fine. I totally understand and I agree."

She pulled her hands away from his and slid the ring off before he could say anything else to cause her imagination to run away with her.

He pulled off his and held his hand out. "I'll stick them both in the cup holder for now."

Leesa nodded, not letting on how she'd kind of wanted to hold onto it. In case they never put them back on, she wanted it as a memory. Something to look at to make her feel bad about what she'd missed out on when she was somewhere else, doing something else. She'd eventually have to figure out where and what that would be one day very soon.

With the rings stowed safely in the truck's console, Chase turned to her. "Okay. Ready?"

She nodded and waited for him to come around and open her door. There were only two other vehicles in the lot. An old rusty truck and a tiny hatchback. She couldn't picture Bruno and the goons arriving in either of those, even if they were trying to be inconspicuous. She relaxed a bit and decided to try and enjoy her night out with Chase. It may be her only one.

Of course the owner knew Chase. The older woman who greeted them, Mrs. Murphy, asked about his family and how long he'd been in town, all the while keeping one eye on Leesa, waiting for an introduction, she supposed. Chase didn't supply Mrs. Murphy with any information, not even when she said, "I'll seat you and your...guest."

"Thank you. I appreciate it." Chase didn't give Mrs. Murphy her adjective of who Leesa was and what she was to Chase.

Once they'd been seated and the owner went through the

kitchen door to get them water and rolls, Leesa smiled. "That just about killed you didn't it?"

"What?" Chase looked up from the single page menu on the table in front of him.

"Not introducing me to her. You're so polite. I could feel how badly you wanted to."

He shook his head, looking horrified. "I am so sorry. I did badly want to introduce you. I just didn't know what to call you."

She knew it. Leesa knew him so well, even though they'd only been together for a few days. "Chase. Honestly. It's okay. I totally understand."

"No, it's not okay. I should have just called you my friend or something. I'll introduce you when she comes back."

Reaching out, she covered his hand with hers. "No. Really. Leave it. It'll give her something to wonder about for a while. Maybe make her slow night go a little faster Besides, I kind of like being mysterious."

Chase let out a snort. "You are mysterious enough already. Believe me."

He squeezed her hand then withdrew his just as Mrs. Murphy came back out. Leesa didn't have time to ask him what he'd meant. Not that she had to. That was probably a conversation better left alone. In fact, once they had rolls, water and had ordered off the menu, Leesa thought it best to change the subject totally.

"Tell me how you started riding."

He glanced up at her. "You really want to know?"

"Of course I do. I mean it's not every day a guy decides to jump on the back of a bull. At least it's not normal where I come from."

"Where do you come from?"

Uh oh. She'd walked right into that one. "A little town no one's ever heard of. But I asked you first. How did you start riding bulls?"

He sighed, looking dissatisfied. "Well, I started riding rough stock when I was in elementary school."

Leesa had no idea what rough stock was, but she didn't care. She knew once Chase started talking about riding, he'd get so absorbed he wouldn't think about anything else, such as where she was from and what she was hiding from him.

She was right. He had started talking and kept going. "I was raised on the farm, and even though we don't have a whole lot of acreage we've always owned a horse or two. I was riding before I was walking. In fact, she doesn't talk about it much, but my mother is a former barrel racer."

"Really." Not sure what exactly a barrel racer did, Leesa nodded suitable encouragement so he would keep talking, which he did.

"We used to go to see the pro rodeo that came through these parts every year. I guess that's what inspired me to want to go pro when I got a little older, but when I was young I just liked it. I started riding bucking stock when I was six. I entered sheep riding contests."

"Sheep? Really?" She pictured a little curly headed, six-year-old Chase hanging onto a sheep and smiled.

"Yeah. It's a good time. You should go to a competition. I'll be riding in a rodeo here in a few weeks. I mean, if you're still here." His eyes dropped.

In a few weeks she'd likely be long gone. That thought made her more determined to enjoy what little time she had left with Chase.

He cleared his throat. "Anyway, I moved on to steers about two years later and worked my way up through the junior ranks. I even qualified for the National High School Rodeo Association. I was on the rodeo team in college. Turns out I was good enough to go pro. I was very lucky. I won Rookie of the Year."

"I somehow don't think luck had much to do with it."

"Thanks." He blushed and she couldn't help but smile.

Meanwhile, she found herself mesmerized by the way his lips looked so sexy. Her gaze dropped to his hands, clasped politely on the table in front of him. She flashed back to all the places they'd been on her body and how good they had felt. She wished she could hold them now, without old lady Murphy seeing them.

"Okay. That's my story. Your turn. How did you end up in Vegas?"

She supposed she could safely tell him part of her story. It might appease him enough he'd stop questioning her about the stuff she couldn't tell. Leesa drew in a deep breath and launched into the tale.

"I was about to go into my senior year of college."

"Where?"

"California." She hoped he wouldn't ask any more questions. In fact, once he'd heard how stupid she was, he probably wouldn't want anything more to do with her. He'd be running to the divorce lawyer and she wouldn't blame him. That would probably be for the best anyway. "I met a guy and was silly enough to believe we were in love and that would be enough."

The full weight of her stupidity hit her hard as she told the story. How she'd dropped out of school after the deadline to get the semester's tuition back that her parents had already paid. It was a considerable sum and she still felt so guilty about it she couldn't bring herself even to voice it out loud.

Leesa glanced at Chase as he watched and waited for her to continue. "Anyway, I left school and followed him to Vegas where he proceeded to run up tens of thousands of dollars worth of credit-card debt. Then he left me with three months worth of back rent to pay."

"He left you?"

She nodded.

"Tell me the credit card wasn't in your name." Chase was leaning forward now.

"Um, sorry. I wish I could." She cringed knowing how absolutely foolish she sounded.

He leaned back in his chair and shook his head. "Wow. What a shithead."

"Yeah." That she could agree with easily.

"What did your parents say?"

"I didn't exactly tell my parents the truth. They think I dropped out of school because I got offered a great job with a huge salary by a corporation in Vegas."

He frowned. "Why would you lie?"

"I'm too embarrassed to tell them the truth. And besides, I figure it won't be a lie one day. If I work hard enough, I can pay off the credit-card debt. Then I'll pay for my last year of school, get my degree and then get that great job they think I already have."

He shot her a doubt-filled look.

"I know. I'm crazy. It seemed like a good idea at the time. First I started temping with a secretarial agency. That was too sporadic and didn't pay that great. So I started waiting tables in a restaurant at one of the casinos. I pretty much sucked at that so my tips were really bad. I was already working the night shift so I thought why not try one of the clubs. I'd talked to one of the other waitresses who'd worked...you know...doing what I ended up doing. She said the money was phenomenal. I figured I could make enough at the club to get out of the hole within a year. But living expenses are so high in Vegas and the interest on my credit cards." She shook her head. "Have you ever looked closely at your statement? The part where it says if you pay the minimum balance you will pay this balance off in thirty-nine years or whatever. It's insane."

"I don't have a credit card."

That stopped her story in mid-flow. "How can you live without a credit card?"

"I have a debit card for hotels and airplane tickets or car rentals. Stuff that needs a card." She considered his credit-less life as he continued. "You don't think you could tell your parents the truth? It would be easier to pay everything off if you moved back home."

"My parents are older. Their health is kind of frail. They don't need my problems on their shoulders." Leesa shook her head. "I can't let them see what I've become."

Chase frowned. "What do you mean, what you've become?"

"You know." Her gaze dropped and she rubbed one fingertip aimlessly over the smooth tabletop.

"Because you worked in a strip club?" Chase kept his voice low. "So what?"

"It's not exactly the profession they paid a fortune in tuition for. It's not something I'm very proud of." Leesa forced herself to look at him, expecting disappointment, but all she saw was sincerity in his eyes.

"Don't you think they'd rather know the truth and have you there with them, than be kept in the dark and separated from you?"

She shook her head. "No. Besides, my older brother lives right down the road from them. With his great job and beautiful wife and perfect children, he can take good care of them. They don't need me there."

Chase's hand covered hers, stilling the idle motion of her fingers.

"You won't have your parents forever you know. If they're old and frail like you say, you're wasting precious time with them."

When she frowned at that Chase rushed on. "I'm not saying that to be mean, Leesa. I'm saying it because it needs to be said. There are no rerides in life."

He'd described what a reride was in the truck, but even if he hadn't the phrase was self-explanatory. She had to admit he was right. "No, there aren't."

"I think if you told them the truth, they'd welcome you back with open arms. Living at home, you could pay your bills off in no time even with working and going to school. I know you can."

She laughed sadly. He made it sound so easy. "You're big on the truth, huh?"

He raised a brow. "I'd like to think everyone is, or at least should be."

"I'm not. You already know I lie to my parents."

Chase shook his head. "You're lying for a good reason. To protect them. I happen to think you're wrong and they could handle the truth, but I understand why you're doing it."

"So lying for a good reason is okay?" She waited for his answer.

"I guess. It's better than lying for a bad reason, but

personally I think telling the truth is still the best course to take."

Leesa nodded. "I know. You're right. I just can't right now."

He nodded. "I understand."

Her gaze met his. "Thanks."

"For what?"

"For being so easy to talk to."

"Well, hell. That's easy." Chase grinned, but his hand held hers more tightly. "You know you can tell me anything. Right?"

He was obviously hoping she'd tell him what exactly she was still hiding.

"I know. Thanks."

Mrs. Murphy returned with their food and once again, they separated before she saw. When she'd gone again, Chase glanced up from his steak. "So this ex boyfriend of yours. He still contact you?"

"No. Thank God." She bit into her hamburger. It was hot and juicy and almost made everything seem right with the world. Kind of like how she felt when she was alone with Chase.

"Good." The single word was said with such resolve, she glanced up at him.

"Would you have beat him up for me if he was still around?"

"Hell yeah. And after I was done, I'm sure a few of my buddies would have wanted a shot too."

She nodded. "Good to know."

That settled it. She could never tell Chase about Jerry, or Bruno, or the two goons, because he'd do exactly what he would have done to her ex. He'd try and take care of it. Only this time, instead of some weak-willed guy who took advantage of girls and then ran away, Chase would be up against an organized-crime syndicate. Way out of his league. The only thing she could do was keep him out of it, and that meant shutting him out of her life.

Suddenly she lost her taste for the burger.

Chapter Fifteen

Chase opened the truck door for Leesa, saw her safely inside, then walked around to the driver's side. She'd opened up to him, more than he'd ever imagined she would actually. Yet there was still something between them. He could feel it. It had been written all over her face as she'd picked at her burger. She was still hiding something. Maybe, eventually, she'd trust him enough to tell him what it was. He only hoped she stuck around long enough for that to happen.

The thought reminded him of the two gold rings lying in the cup holder between their two seats. He reached down in the dim light of the parking lot and picked them up. Holding those rings gave him such mixed feelings. They made him feel both warm and sad at the same time. While she wore it, he knew she wouldn't leave. The minute they were legally no longer bound, he felt certain she'd be gone. He could see that in her eyes too.

After feeling for the larger ring, he slid it back onto his finger. He held out his hand toward her. "Left hand, please."

She did as he asked. He slipped the smaller of the two bands onto her fourth finger. She stared down at it for a second, then her gaze moved to his face. "Is there somewhere we can go?"

"Sure. Like where? There's a movie theater in town. I'm not sure what's playing or what time—"

"I mean to be alone."

His eyes opened with the realization. "Oh."

He couldn't get the truck started fast enough. Once he had, he backed them out of the space and headed out of town to a place where they could be alone. He hadn't been there in a few years, and he wouldn't dare tell Leesa he'd been there at all. Girls could get jealous about stuff like that. It was silly actually, because he had a feeling if he could only get her to trust him and stick around, Leesa could be the last girl he'd ever want to take parking at the lake.

They arrived in record time, mostly due to his speeding. The moment he turned off the ignition, she was in his lap.

With her mouth covering his, and her straddling him in the tight space between his body and the steering wheel, he somehow managed to reach down and slide the seat back farther. It still didn't give them a whole lot of room, but she didn't seem to care.

She kissed him like it was the last time. He pushed that thought out of his head quickly. Uncle Gary wasn't even back from his case yet. They had time together. At least a week. Not that a week would ever be enough.

Leesa reached between them for his belt buckle and thoughts of his uncle fled only to be replaced by how he was going to reach into his pocket for the condom he'd stashed there just in case.

As she worked on getting his jeans open in the close quarters, he had no problem sliding his hands beneath her dress. Dresses were marvelous things. Women should wear them all the time. He had a handful of smooth warm flesh, and he hadn't had to work very hard to find it, unlike Leesa who was still struggling with his jeans button. He could have helped her, but he decided to enjoy touching her first. He dipped a finger beneath the elastic of her underwear. She drew in a sharp breath. He explored her further and found her hot wet core.

Chase was glad he was still trapped inside his pants because it was too tempting to slide inside her. First he wanted to give her a time she'd never forget.

A bed would be so nice right now, but that was not in the cards. He'd have to limit himself to what he'd been given. His finger found and worked the spot guaranteed to make her squirm. He worked it until she was trembling against him. Then he worked it some more until she cried out and clung to him like he was the only lifeline she had in the world.

"There's a condom in my pocket." He spoke against her ear and she shivered.

"Get it." Her voice was breathless.

He claimed her mouth again, not nearly done with her yet. She moved back enough for him to wiggle his hand into his pocket and pull out the packet. She took it from him, tearing it open with her teeth, as if she couldn't open it fast enough. With a grin, he reached down and freed himself from his jeans and boxers. It wasn't going to be perfect with him half in his jeans and the steering wheel pressing into Leesa's back, but he was with her and alone, and that was good enough.

Once she covered him and he slid into her, he couldn't have cared if they were standing on hot coals. He wouldn't have noticed. All he felt was how tight and hot it felt to be inside her. The only thing he cared about was that they fit together perfectly. That her body responded to his like they'd been made for each other.

He could easily do this every day, twice a day, and never get tired of it, of her. If only she'd let him.

She moved faster over him, and he buried his head against

her chest, breathing in the scent of her. She smelled of a combination of the soap his mother kept in the shower and something that was uniquely her.

He held her tightly to him as her hips moved, taking him to new heights. He didn't want to finish and leave her, and he didn't think she'd be willing to stick around for round two considering they were parked where another car could possibly drive by and see them. He held on until her body began to grip his. Chase felt her come and couldn't hold back any longer.

They clung to each other and Chase vowed he was going to do whatever it took to convince this girl to stay in his life.

He came to that realization just as she laughed in his arms.

Chase pulled back to look into her face. "You're going to give me a complex laughing while I'm still inside you."

"Sorry, but your pants are vibrating."

Now that she mentioned it, he felt it too. "I put my phone on vibrate while we were in the restaurant. I'm sorry."

"It's okay. You want to answer it?"

He was still buried deep inside the woman in his lap and he had no desire to leave, in spite of the fact he was fading fast and would have no choice in the matter very soon. Still the answer was clear. "No."

She laughed. "You never answer it."

"I do when I'm not occupied with someone much more interesting than whoever is on that call." With that he nibbled on her neck and felt her sigh against him. "I will definitely answer any time you call me."

He only hoped that she would. Then something odd struck him. "Do you have a cell phone? I've never seen you with one."

"I, uh, lost it recently. I didn't have time to replace it." She pulled back from him and started to get off his lap. He knew immediately there was much more to her story than she'd revealed.

He had to deal with cleaning himself up so he didn't try and stop her when she moved back to her own seat. Besides, he had run out of ideas of how he could get her to confide in him. He guessed she needed time. Unfortunately, time was not something he had a lot of.

After fastening his pants and belt again, he turned in the seat to face her. He laid his head against the head rest and simply took in the vision of Leesa, freshly loved and still a little breathless.

She smiled and broke eye contact. "You make me nervous when you look at me like that."

"Nothing to be nervous about. I just like looking at you. Did I tell you how beautiful you look tonight?"

The truck was only lit with the pale glow of moonlight, but he would make a bet she blushed. She was a woman who didn't like getting compliments, but he intended to keep giving them to her until she got used to it.

"I don't, but thank you."

"You do. And that dress suits you perfectly."

"It does. Thank you again for that and for dinner." She laughed. "It seems like I owe you a lot."

He leaned closer and took her hand in his. He fingered the ring on her finger. "Yeah? Hmm. I guess I'll have to come up with a way for you to pay me back."

She shook her head but smiled. "Oh really. What do you have in mind?"

"I'll think of something. Ready to go home?"

Leesa nodded. "Yes. Do I look all right? I mean will your family know what we've been doing?"

Chase laughed. "Cody is going to assume it whether we did it or not. My parents are going to hope we never have and they'll turn a blind eye just to keep believing that. And we'd be lucky if Christine noticed if the house was on fire the way she's so involved in her television. So no, I wouldn't worry. I think our secret is safe as far as the family goes."

"I'm glad. I like your family."

His hand paused on the key and he glanced at her. "Good."

Maybe they would be one more thing to sway her to stay in his life. He started the truck and headed for home.

It was hard saying goodnight to Leesa at the door of his room when all he wanted to do was pick her up and toss her onto the bed. But he managed it and then went to his temporary quarters in Cody's room.

Luckily Cody was out, so he had some privacy to think about everything. All Leesa had told him. All that he was sure she hadn't. It was also nice to think back on their time at the lake without being under Cody's scrutiny. Chase emptied his pockets and remembered the missed call on his cell phone. It had been Garret again. He flipped it open and noticed there was a message this time. Feeling guilty for dodging the calls, Chase punched in his code and listened. Garret was probably good and pissed by now he hadn't been answering.

"Chase, man, I'm sorry. Okay? It was just a little joke. It's nothing to stop talking to me over though. Call me back."

He frowned. What was just a joke? He hit the button and waited for the ring and then for Garret's voice. "Chase. Hey."

"What was just a joke?"

"You don't know? Why haven't you been picking up your phone if you're not mad at me?"

A feeling of doom descended, settling smack in the middle of his chest. "Garret. Tell me. What joke?"

"The rings. The fake marriage license and receipt."

Chase swallowed hard. "What are you talking about?" He hoped against hope he wasn't hearing what he'd just heard.

"Didn't you take all that stuff with you when you left? When we found it and you gone and you wouldn't answer your phone, I figured you were mad."

"Just tell me exactly what you did." His heart was pounding now and the steak threatened to come back up.

"When you and that girl fell asleep so early, Skeeter and I thought it would be funny to play a little joke on you. We went down to the gift shop and bought a novelty marriage license and two cheap rings. Then it was Skeeter's idea to make up one of those tear off receipts to make it look more authentic. You know those receipts like waitresses use when they take your order at a diner or whatever. So we asked one of the cocktail waitresses for a blank one and we made up a receipt. We didn't mean to get you mad though. We just thought it would be funny."

Chase dropped down onto Cody's bed and buried his face in his hand. It still didn't make sense though. "How did you get our signatures?"

"Dude, how many autograph signings have we been to together? I mean I could forge your signature blindfolded."

"What about Leesa's?"

"Yeah, that I feel kind of bad about, but it was actually Skeeter's idea so you can get mad at him too. Her wallet was lying on top of her duffle bag. We opened it and got out her driver's license and copied the signature from there. I'm sorry about that. We shouldn't have gone through her stuff, but we were kinda drunk. You know?"

Chase drew in a shaky breath. "Yeah. I know."

He'd just lost any hope of keeping her around and found out he'd been living a lie thinking he was married for the past few days. It hadn't been very long at all, but knowing it wasn't true...he almost felt like he was mourning the loss of it. It had been real to them.

Thank God he hadn't gone to his uncle with some novelty marriage certificate forged by his two drunk friends. It was bad enough he'd have to confess it all to his parents. And worse, tell Leesa.

Then what? He dreaded even thinking of that.

"Chase. I'm really sorry."

"It's all right. I'm not mad."

"Okay. Good. So what's up? What have you been doing? Ooo, what happened with that girl? You left so fast the next day and I haven't gotten to talk to you."

It was back to business as usual with Garret. He had no idea what news he'd just delivered to Chase and how it had affected him.

Cody walked through the door. He only had to look at Chase's face before he frowned. He mouthed, "What's wrong?"

"Listen, Garret. My brother just got home and I gotta talk to him. I'll call you back later. Okay?"

"Yeah, sure. Later."

Chase hit the button to disconnect the call and sat, phone still in his hand.

"What happened? Did one of the guys get hurt?"

"No." The question shook Chase out of his shock. Finally he shut the phone and tossed it onto the dresser. He glanced down at his hand and let out a sad laugh. "I'm not married."

"The divorce went through that fast?"

"No. We were never married. The guys were playing a practical joke on me." He pulled the ring off and tossed it next to the phone. "It was all a big joke."

"This is good news, bro. Now you don't have all the divorce stuff to go through. You two can just date like normal people."

Chase shook his head. "I'm not sure Leesa wants that."

"Did you ask her?"

"No."

Cody threw his hands up in the air. "Then how can you know that?"

"I don't know. I just do."

"Well, you're going to have to tell her the truth."

"I know." Chase ran his hands through his hair. Could he put it off until tomorrow? Not that he'd get any sleep tonight. "Maybe she's sleeping already."

Cody frowned at the clock. "It's a little early for her to be sleeping."

He didn't even have to look at the clock to know that was true. He'd just said good night to Leesa and left her at the door. "Yeah. I know."

"Putting it off isn't going to do any good."

Chase knew that was true, but putting it off felt better. At least it gave him a little time. He got up. "All right."

"Good luck. And ask her."

"I will." Like a man walking to his execution, Chase headed out the door.

The hallway had never seemed so short. Before he knew it, he was standing in front of his bedroom. Leesa's bedroom. He raised his fist and knocked softly. He heard her footsteps inside and pictured her adorable feet. Then the door was open.

He leaned against the doorframe. "Hi."

"Hi." She was still in the dress she'd worn to dinner.

She'd only owned it for a few hours, but he already had very fond memories of that dress. He tried not to think of that. It was only making this harder. "We need to talk."

"Um, okay." She backed away from the door. "Do you want to come in?"

"Yeah. Thanks." He walked in and closed the door behind him.

To hell with his parents' rule. Like Cody said, it was still early and they needed to talk in private. His mother and father would have to deal with it. He was an adult, after all. They both were. "Um, so I talked to Garret."

"Good. I felt bad you kept ditching his calls."

Chase laughed, wishing he'd ditched him one more time and not listened to the voicemail.

"He told me something." This was turning out to be harder than he'd anticipated. "Sit down."

Leesa frowned but perched on the edge of the bed. "Okay. I'm sitting."

He found himself glancing at the ring on her finger. At the same time, he felt the smooth ringless skin on his own. "It was a practical joke. We didn't wander down to the chapel drunk or sleepwalking or whatever. Garret and Skeeter forged our names on some souvenir marriage license they found in the gift shop."

"What?" She shook her head like she was trying to comprehend it.

"We're not married. We never were." She had no idea how much it pained him to say that.

"Oh." She glanced down at her ring and laughed sadly. "I guess I should take this off then."

His heart jumped. He walked to the bed and kneeled in front of her. Taking her hands in his, he pulled the ring off her left hand and slid it onto her right. "How about you wear it here? I know it's not a fancy ring but…"

"It'll give me something to remember us by." Her voice was so soft he barely heard it. He wished he hadn't. That wasn't exactly the finish to his sentence he had been hoping for. What Chase wanted was for her not to go far enough to have to remember him, because he'd be right there.

"I guess we should tell your parents now." Her gaze met his. "How do you think they're going to take this piece of news?"

"After the last announcement we made, I can't imagine anything I say now will shock them. I'll handle it though. It was my stupid friends who did this, and my fault I drank enough I slept so hard I didn't hear them doing it. I'll deal with it. Besides, my daddy will likely have a few choice words to say about Garret and Skeeter, and I'm not sure they'll be fit for a lady."

She smiled, but it managed to have sadness in it. "I've heard pretty much everything, but okay. You can handle it."

Chase nodded. "There's something else."

"What else could there possibly be?"

"Well, now that we don't have to deal with a wedding we didn't remember and a divorce we weren't sure how to go about getting, I figure we might have time to just date each other. Tonight was a really good start." Oh boy had it been. He wouldn't mind a few repeats of it and soon. "What do you think? We were pretty good at being married. I'd like to see if we're good at being a couple."

He waited for her answer, still holding on to her hands tightly.

"There is nothing I'd like more."

He didn't understand the tears that filled her eyes, but her answer made him more than happy. "Good."

Chase dropped a kiss on her mouth. It was meant to be a quick one, but it somehow became more. Perhaps it was Leesa's hands tangled in his hair as she kissed him until they were both breathless. Maybe it was just that he couldn't ever seem to get enough of her.

He broke away. "If I don't leave now, I'm never leaving, and I think Mama and Daddy might object to that. Especially now that we're not even temporarily married."

She nodded, her eyes still glassy with what he hoped were tears of happiness. They should have plenty to be happy about. He'd asked her to be his girlfriend, she'd said yes and they didn't have to go through the divorce.

One day he'd figure out women. He'd enjoy figuring Leesa out.

Chapter Sixteen

Leesa didn't sleep. She knew she wouldn't. This was it. It was over. Time to leave. There was nothing left keeping her here besides her pointless desire to be Chase's girlfriend and see where things went with them.

She couldn't do that. Not with Jerry after her, and staying any longer under false pretences was wrong. She couldn't stay with Chase just because she felt safer hiding here. Besides, what if she was wrong and Jerry's guys knew exactly where she was and were just biding their time. Waiting for the perfect opportunity to, she didn't know, blow up the house with her and all of Chase's family in it. She couldn't take that risk.

She'd watched the odometer in his truck on the drive to town. It was only about a mile. She had seen a pay phone at the gas station. She could call information and get a cab from the next town over maybe. It could take her to the nearest bus station. That would put a considerable dent in her spending money but what else could she do?

Leesa waited until the house was silent. She'd never actually unpacked her bag. She'd been kind of living out of it, knowing she wouldn't be staying long. That didn't make going any easier though. She considered leaving the dress Chase had bought her but decided that was silly. It wasn't like he could return it. She'd already worn it. She folded it and the sweater and put it neatly on top of the rest of her things, then laid the new shoes he'd bought her on top and pulled the zipper shut.

Now for the hard part. She sat at Chase's desk and pulled open a drawer. Being a boy's desk, there was everything in the drawer, from an old metal toy truck that probably dated back a good fifteen years, to a few awards for his riding. Leesa eventually found a pencil. Holding it up, she saw teeth marks and smiled. She pictured a younger Chase doing his homework, chewing on the pencil as he thought about whatever problem he was working on. With that pencil, she wrote the hardest letter she'd ever written, then left his room and didn't look back.

She was back in her sneakers and sweatshirt again, but given the cool night, and with a mile to walk, she was grateful for that. She'd at least gotten to do a load of laundry, so her pitifully small wardrobe was clean. With that small happy thought which was outweighed a million fold by the sadness in her heart, she slipped out the back door and started walking.

The night was clear. It was kind of peaceful actually, with not a car on the road. Just the sound of the night in the country. Leesa hadn't heard that in a long time. The hoot of an owl. The scampering of little furry feet in the woods along the road. She reached the pay phone without seeing another living soul. Leesa wasn't sure if she should find that comforting or scary.

After letting her bag drop heavily to the ground, she rotated her shoulder and tried to work out the stiffness there. She hoped she'd be able to get a taxi or it was going to be a long walk ahead. She rummaged in her pocket and pulled out her wallet. Inside, she found an old calling card that still had some minutes on it. Without her cell phone, this would have to do for now.

Leesa imagined where that phone might be now. Could she

even dare report it lost and have it deactivated? Of course not. That would tip Jerry off to her location. She sighed. Vegas had defeated her. She'd never get out of the hole she was in. She'd never be able to go home to her parents as the success she pretended to be.

She should call them now, on her way out of town. If the bad guys had a trace on her parents' phone, she'd be long gone by the time they got here looking for her, hopefully on a bus heading somewhere else.

Leesa steeled herself to dial her parents' number. It wasn't too late to call the West Coast. They'd be sitting in their chairs, side by side, watching one of their shows on television. They'd stay up for the eleven o'clock news so they could check the weather for the next day, then go to bed. She'd never been able to convince them that they could get a computer and see the weather on there. Or even watch the weather channel any time of day or night and get the local forecast. They were creatures of habit. Maybe that was why they believed her lies so readily. They were simply used to trusting her. Leesa's lying was a recent addition to her repertoire.

Her mom would answer after the first ring. The phone, an ancient looking one, the kind that still had a cord attached to the wall, had always sat on the table between their two chairs. An easy reach for either one of them, though her mother was usually the one to answer.

Every word Chase had said over dinner replayed in Leesa's head as she changed her mind about calling her parents and hung up the receiver. She didn't want to lie to them anymore, but she also couldn't tell them the truth right now.

Maybe if Jerry and his brother weren't in the picture things could be different. She could go home and tell them everything. As things stood, it was safer to stay away. She didn't know what she'd do or where'd she'd end up eventually, but at least she knew her next move. She had to get out of here.

This was a small town. There was even a phone book where one was supposed to be. She flipped through the pages, looking first for public transportation and then for a taxi company close by but not from this town. Chase would have probably gone to school with the driver if she chose a company from here. She didn't want him to be the laughing stock of the locals or pitied either, that the girl he'd had dinner with snuck out on him in the middle of the night. She also didn't want to risk him tracking her down and trying to follow her. The situation was both too dangerous and too painful for her to see him again.

Selection made, Leesa marked the toll free listing for the cab company with one finger and picked up the receiver. Time to get on with her life.

Leesa wiped her hands on the polyester apron tied around her waist and tried to remember why she'd walked back into the kitchen. Her weary brain finally supplied the answer as she stared into the reach-in fridge and frowned. Catsup for table eight.

"Here's your tip from table twelve, Leesa. Raul bussed it and I wiped it down for you. You just have to reset."

"Thanks, Tina." Once again her coworkers were picking up her slack. Leesa pocketed the two single dollar bills and sighed. At this rate she'd have her bills paid off in about fifty years or so.

The redhead paused in what seemed like her usual state of constant motion. "You know. You'd make more tips if you gave them a little something extra."

"Something extra?" Leesa nearly laughed. Déjà vu of an

eerily similar conversation with Holly not even a month ago struck her. She waited for Tina's theory on getting larger tips, not sure she wanted to hear it after what had happened the last time.

"You know, nothing that will be noticed. Like cut them a really large piece of pie once in a while. Or refill their soda for free even though there's only free refills on coffee and iced tea," Tina continued.

"Okay. Thanks. I'll keep that in mind." Leesa let out a huge sigh.

"You all right?"

She nodded. "Yeah. Just tired."

"You can go if you want. It's pretty dead out there. I can handle it alone."

Leesa knew that was true. She probably only got in everyone's way. No wonder Tina was anxious for her to go home. "You sure?"

"Yup. Not a problem."

Who was she to argue? It wasn't like she was making good tips anyway. Leesa held up the bottle she'd just grabbed. "I better get this to table eight, then I guess I'll reset table twelve and go."

Already halfway back to her table with their food, Tina dismissed her with a quickly waved goodbye.

Leesa needed to call her parents anyway. It had been two weeks since she'd talked to them.

She tried not to feel guilty about how seldom she could call home as she rode the bus to a town half an hour away. She'd spotted a pay phone outside the library the last time she'd been there using the computers and internet. Next week she'd have to go to a different town with a different library and hopefully find a working pay phone there as well. If Jerry had her parents' phone tapped, she couldn't safely come back to this town again.

She'd gotten so used to taking the bus that it seemed like no time before she was dialing her parents' phone number. Leesa stashed the anxiety of the past few weeks away temporarily. Donning a smile since she was convinced her mother could hear it in her voice, she said, "Hey, Mom. It's me."

"Leesa. Where are you?" That was not her mother's usual greeting.

"I'm uh, traveling again for work. Why? Is something wrong?" Panic hit her hard. For the first time in weeks, Leesa tasted the fear she'd felt when fleeing Vegas.

The image of Bruno with a gun pressed against her mother's head nearly took her off her feet.

"Two men were here looking for you..."

Leesa swayed and grabbed for the shelf beneath the phone to stop herself from falling. Tiny black spots began to close in on the edges of her vision.

"...they left their number and said that if I heard from you, I should have you call them. Leesa, they said they were from the FBI."

Jerry's guys were pretending to be FBI now. They were still trying to find her, but they hadn't harmed her parents. Not yet. That was what was important. She tried to compose herself. "Okay. What's the number?"

Even though she had no intention of calling it, she scribbled down the number with shaky hands on her order pad still in the apron shoved in her bag. She had to get off the phone so she could go vomit somewhere and then figure out what to do. "Thanks, Mom. I'll call them."

"Leesa. What's this about? Why would the FBI need to talk

to you?"

A suitable lie didn't present itself, and she couldn't tell her mother it most likely wasn't the FBI but rather the two men hired to kill her, so she did the best she could. She told the truth for once. "I don't know, Mom. I'll call you again soon. Love you."

Leesa slammed the receiver down, as if hanging up extra hard would stop any phone trace or wire tap more quickly than disconnecting the call normally. Shaking so hard she could barely read the number she'd written down, she stared at the piece of paper in her hand. What should she do? What if it really had been the FBI looking for her?

She needed to take another risk, one she hoped would pay off. It took her two times to dial in Holly's cell phone number correctly, but Leesa finally heard her old friend's voice answer. Thank goodness she didn't get voice mail.

"Holly. It's Leesa. If you're at work or not alone, don't let on it's me. Okay?"

"Leesa. Oh my God. Do you have any idea what's been happening here?"

"No. Tell me."

"Jerry turned state's evidence and then disappeared. His brother is in jail and the club's been shut down."

"What? Holly, slow down. Tell me what happened exactly."

"It all went down right after you left. There was some FBI sting happening right under our noses. One of the guys Jerry was meeting with was an undercover fed. Apparently they got enough evidence to arrest Jerry. The minute they did, he sang like a bird and spilled everything he knew, including financial records of all the money his brother was laundering through the club. Meanwhile, every employee had to give a statement to the feds and the club has been shut down."

For the second time in just a few minutes, Leesa grabbed the shelf for support. Maybe it really had been the FBI looking for her. The FBI visiting her parents now made perfect sense. They probably needed her statement, but that didn't mean Jerry's hit wasn't still on. "Where is Jerry now?"

"Gone. We figure they got him in witness protection until the trial. Word is his brother is pissed."

She could imagine Johnny would be far more pissed at his brother than he was at her having seen the back of a man sitting at a desk with money in front of him. In fact, that man she'd seen was probably the undercover agent.

"Wow." That was all Leesa could manage at the moment, she was in such shock.

"Where are you? Are you okay?"

Leesa had been on the run too long to answer the first question willingly, but she answered the second. "Yeah, I'm fine."

Jerry and his brother were both out of commission now and probably too worried about staying alive themselves to worry about her. Leesa knew a little something about being consumed with trying to stay alive.

If what Holly said was true, Leesa could go back to Vegas, but then what? Her rent was paid through the end of the month. She could get the rest of her stuff out and move home. Or stay and go back to stripping.

Her life might almost be normal again, but all of the old problems that existed before were still there. She was still lying to her parents. And Chase... Did she dare hope to build something with him after how she'd left things?

"Are you coming back? I found a job at a new club on the strip. I can put in a good word for you."

Thinking of Chase and the short time she'd had with him seemed to make everything clear for her. Suddenly Leesa knew with certainty going back to stripping in Vegas was one thing she wouldn't be doing. "No. I'll be back to clean up some loose ends, but no. I think I'll be moving back home for a bit. At least until I get my life together again."

"Good. I think that's a good idea."

Leesa nodded. "Yeah, I think so too."

Chapter Seventeen

The bull ran into the chute. Chase dropped to his knee and said the usual prayer, asking God to protect both himself and this animal from harm during his ride.

Antsy, the bull rattled the rails as Chase climbed over the top. His brother was there right behind the chute, delivering encouragement with his words and his very presence. One reason Chase liked riding close to home was his family being there. Even though this wasn't the professional bull riding championship series, but rather a local rodeo he'd chosen to ride in, having loved ones close meant a lot. Particularly now, when he needed all the support he could find to ease the hurt Leesa had left behind.

He knew he needed to concentrate on the ride, not on memories of her. Yet the letter she'd left behind still popped into his head at the worst times, like now for instance.

I can't stay. No explanation as to why.

It's best if we don't talk again. Please don't try to contact me.

Meanwhile, Chase was about to compete for the first time since she left and he had his wedding ring in his pocket. The superstitious riders back on tour would be crossing themselves and sending up extra prayers if they knew that.

It wouldn't be the gold band in his jeans that got him hurt, but it might be his lack of concentration. Trying his best to center his mind, Chase lowered himself onto the bull's back and slid his gloved fingers into the bull rope's handle. He pulled and then wrapped the rope tight around his hand. Flexing his fingers a few times, he tested the wrap.

The bull made one single but powerful move and crashed forward against the front of the chute. Bearing down with his legs, Chase lowered his chin, raised his arm and nodded to the gate man. Then they were off into the arena.

The bull went into a perfect spin into Chase's hand, bucking just enough to impress the four judges but not enough to send Chase into the dirt. Just the kind of ride he liked.

He knew the announcer's voice filled the arena above the cheers from the crowd, but the only sound Chase focused on was the eight-second buzzer. When he heard that, he took the safest way off the animal. He pulled the tail of the rope to release his hand and threw his left leg over the animal's head. He jumped off the side, then felt his right foot catch.

His head slammed into the dirt as his spur got momentarily caught in the flank strap. He was vaguely aware of the shouts of the bullfighters as hooves came down close to his face. Chase pulled himself into a ball, squeezed his eyes shut and waited for the pain, but it never came.

His head was spinning and he was sure he'd have a headache from hell later, but that was all. The bull was out of the arena and hands were lifting him from the dirt. Still dizzy, he took the help from the medical team to get off the ground. Once he assured them he was fine, and let them shine a light in his eyes, they let him walk out of the arena under his own steam, which was always a good thing.

He was greeted behind the chutes by smiling faces and more than one hand pounding him on the back.

"Great ride, man."

"Perfect ride. You're in the lead."

Chase accepted the congratulations from the other riders with a nod as his brother ran up to him.

"Holy shit, Chase. Did you see your score?"

Pulling the mouth guard from his mouth, he shook his head. "No."

He looked for the scoreboard but hadn't located it yet thanks to what may well be a concussion when his brother supplied the information. "Ninety and a quarter."

Normally, Chase would have jumped for joy at that information, but right now there was only one thing he could comprehend. That was Leesa pushing her way through the crowd as she came toward him. Even more amazingly, she was wearing the dress he'd bought for her.

Cody didn't see her since she was behind him, but Chase couldn't take his eyes off her.

"You okay?" Cody put a hand on his shoulder and blocked his view of Leesa as he peered into Chase's eyes. "You might have a concussion."

"I'm fine." Chase pushed his brother's hand away and moved to look around him.

Cody finally turned just as Leesa, teary eyed, reached them.

"Ah." He glanced at Chase and raised a brow. "Do you want me to stay or go?"

It was a valid question. Cody had been on the receiving end of Chase's mood swings for the past few weeks. They'd had some good sparring sessions because of them though. Chase found it helpful to beat the crap out of something when trying to heal a broken heart. Here before him stood the cause of that pain, but all he could think as his pulse raced was that she'd come back to him.

"You can go." He spoke to Cody, but his eyes never left Leesa, who was crying openly now.

"I saw you fall. Are you hurt?" Her voice quavered.

"That? Nah. That was nothing." He reached out and she came willingly into his arms. Burying his face in her hair, he squeezed her tightly to him and tried to absorb that she was really there. He was holding her again when he thought he never would.

"I'm so sorry." Her apology was muffled, delivered into the vest he hadn't yet taken off after his ride.

"It's okay." He rubbed her back, as much for her comfort as for his own. Maybe if he touched her enough he'd start to believe she was really back.

Her tearstained face lifted. "I have so much to tell you."

His relief over that statement nearly brought tears to his own eyes. "Okay."

"After I tell you, once I explain, maybe you'll be able to forgive me."

Hurt and confused as he was, he'd never been able to be angry with her. He pulled back far enough to slide his right hand into the front pocket of his jeans. He brought out the ring he'd worn for those few short days when they'd thought they were married.

"I'll listen, and I'll be happy to hear whatever you are willing to tell me, but there's nothing to forgive. You're here and that's good enough for me."

When she saw what he was holding, her expression turned hopeful and amazed at the same time. "You're carrying it with you?"

"Yeah, I am." More than just carrying it. He'd ridden with it on him. She had no idea the significance of that.

"How can you be so perfect?"

Chase laughed. "My family would disagree with you."

"Then I'll have to fight them on this. Chase Reese, you are the most amazing person I've ever met."

He smiled and, staring into the face he'd never been able to get out of his mind, brushed a hair from her cheek. "Ditto."

She reached up and grabbed his hand, holding it to her face like she was afraid to let him go.

The glint of gold on her finger caught his eye. He swallowed past the lump in his throat. "You're still wearing yours."

"I never took it off." Her eyes glistened as she stared up at him.

Chase laced his fingers through hers. He wasn't one to give orders, especially to a lady, but he'd waited too long for her already. "We're gonna go someplace private, you're gonna tell me what you have to, then we're gonna talk about you and me and how we're gonna make this work. Got it?"

She nodded. "Got it."

He lowered his head. "I'm not letting you get away from me again."

"Okay."

"You don't have a problem with that, do you?"

"No." She smiled and then laughed.

Chase narrowed his eyes playfully. "You laughing at me, woman?"

"No, sir. I just think I like this new forceful side of you."

"Good. Now come on. That was my last ride until tomorrow. We can disappear and no one will notice."

"Chase?"

"Yeah."

"Do you think after we talk we can take a ride in the truck?"

He smiled, hoping she had in mind what he did, which was confirmed when she added. "You know, I am in a dress."

"So I see. It'd be a shame to waste it."

"Exactly."

He lowered his head and tasted what he'd been missing, what he'd been dreaming about. Behind her back, he slipped the ring onto the fourth finger of his right hand. There it would stay for the time being anyway, because with this woman in his arms and back in his life, his left hand ring finger was feeling awfully naked.

About the Author

As an award-winning author of contemporary erotic romance in genres including military, cowboy, ménage and paranormal, Cat Johnson uses her computer so much she wore the letters off the keyboard within a year. She is known for her creative marketing and research practices. Consequently, Cat owns an entire collection of camouflage shoes for book signings and a fair number of her consultants wear combat or cowboy boots for a living. In her real life, she's been a marketing manager, professional harpist, bartender, tour guide, radio show host, Junior League president, sponsor of a bull riding rodeo cowboy, wife and avid animal lover.

To learn more about Cat, please visit www.catjohnson.net. Send an email to Cat at cat@catjohnson.net, friend her on Myspace at www.myspace.com/authorcatjohnson or follow her on Twitter at www.twitter.com/cat_johnson.

The best way to heal a broken heart is to jump right back on the horse. So to speak...

Jack

© 2010 Cat Johnson

Red, Hot & Blue, Book 2

After watching the girl he's crushed on for years fall for his best friend, the last thing special operative Jack Gordon wants is a vacation. If cooling his heels doesn't drive him crazy, doing it under his family's scrutiny will.

But once he's back home things get more than a little interesting. The new farm hand is cute, sexy—and his instincts tell him she's got something to hide. Luckily, he's got the skills and the backup to find out what.

Gordon Equine is the perfect place for Niccolina Campolini. The Gordons pay in room, board and cash. And they don't ask questions. Perfect for a girl on the run...until Jack shows up. Sexy as hell and far too inquisitive, Jack strikes sparks and suspicions that put both her body and her heart in danger.

Jack knows better than to trust a woman with as many shadows as Nicki, but the heat waves of their attraction are messing with his focus. And when her secrets catch up with her, he's not sure if he's protecting her from something, or protecting his family from her...

Warning: This book contains extremely stupid gangsters bearing guns, a bored team of special operatives looking for some action, and one Southern gentleman guaranteed to charm your panties off.

Available now in ebook and print from Samhain Publishing.

When the going gets tough, the tough get busy. Real busy.

Breaking Brent
© *2010 Niki Green*
Roped, Book 2

In Millbrook, Texas, there are cowboys. Then there are the Kiels, every girl's idea of perfection in tight-fittin' jeans. Peyton James is no different. Only she doesn't want to admit it—because three years ago Brent Kiel ripped out her heart and handed it back in teeny little pieces.

In a twist of fate Peyton wound up engaged to Brent's best friend. The engagement might be off now, but no one needs to know, right? It keeps the questions at bay...and the temptation called Brent Kiel out of reach. Until the night he shows up at her family's bar.

The only reason Brent agrees to meet his brothers at Big Jack's is that Peyton never darkens the door on a Friday night. Except tonight. Seeing her is a painful reminder of his mistake and what it cost him—and that no other woman's lips or body will ever satisfy him like hers.

Nothing—not the past, not her legendary temper, not even the rock on her finger—will keep this cowboy from getting what he wants...

Warning: Seduction served by a brooding and standoffish cowboy who wants nothing more than his ladylove's heart and soul—her body is just icing on the cake. Hot cowboy sex in a bar, in a barn, in a bed...just about anywhere.

Available now in ebook and print from Samhain Publishing.

GREAT
CHEAP
FUN

Discover eBooks!

CPSIA information can be obtained at www.ICGtesting.com
Printed in the USA
LVOW060009271012

304633LV00001B/138/P